Ellis waited a few minutes
back on track before he s
how come you were out b
a Friday night anyway? I
club bouncers would have seen
enough to not hassle you."

T0009973

Galen reached for a larger screwdriver from the tool cart behind him. "Sick of the clubs. Have been for a while. Ben and Joe still like the whole Townsend-playboy thing, but I guess I'm lazy or something. It's too much work for a one-night stand." And wasn't it weird his deepest secret tumbled right off his lips to a near-total stranger.

"Or you want someone to stick around for more than one night. I get it. Someone who likes you when you're just kicking back doing your own thing. Talk books, work on the car, build stuff…." Ellis paused long enough that Galen looked up, and sure enough, those browless eyes did a great imitation of eyebrows waggling. "Spend all day in various erotic and possibly gymnastic endeavors."

Dammit, he never had outgrown the epic blush. Galen felt it flare from the tips of his ears clear down to his navel. The frog's not-frogish chuckle didn't help at all.

"Got you thinking, didn't I?" Ellis left his makeshift pond and hopped over next to Galen's tools. "God, that's a pretty blush. Wanna try another kiss?"

"Or I could wait until nine tonight and kiss you for real." His mind—ignoring the whole *total stranger* thing again—had wandered right into those images anyway, tangling his fingers in pale strands and pulling that long body close to his….

DREAMSPUN
BEYOND

Dear Reader,

Love is the dream. It dazzles us, makes us stronger, and brings us to our knees. Dreamspun Desires tell stories of love featuring your favorite heartwarming heroes, captivating plots, and exotic locations. Stories that make your breath catch and your imagination soar.

In the pages of these wonderful love stories, readers can escape to a world where love conquers all, the tenderness of a first kiss sweeps you away, and your heart pounds at the sight of the one you love.

When you put it all together, you find romance in its truest form.

Love always finds a way.

Elizabeth North

Executive Director
Dreamspinner Press

Terry Wylis

KISSING FROGS

DREAMSPUN
BEYOND

PUBLISHED BY

DREAMSPINNER
PRESS

Published by
DREAMSPINNER PRESS

5032 Capital Circle SW, Suite 2, PMB# 279,
Tallahassee, FL 32305-7886 USA
www.dreamspinnerpress.com

This is a work of fiction. Names, characters, places, and incidents either
are the product of author imagination or are used fictitiously, and any
resemblance to actual persons, living or dead, business establishments,
events, or locales is entirely coincidental.

Kissing Frogs
© 2023 Terry Wylis

Cover Art
© 2023 L.C. Chase
http://www.lcchase.com
Cover content is for illustrative purposes only and any person depicted
on the cover is a model.

All rights reserved. This book is licensed to the original purchaser only.
Duplication or distribution via any means is illegal and a violation of
international copyright law, subject to criminal prosecution and upon
conviction, fines, and/or imprisonment. Any eBook format cannot be le-
gally loaned or given to others. No part of this book may be reproduced
or transmitted in any form or by any means, electronic or mechanical,
including photocopying, recording, or by any information storage and
retrieval system, without the written permission of the Publisher, except
where permitted by law. To request permission and all other inquiries,
contact Dreamspinner Press, 5032 Capital Circle SW, Suite 2, PMB#
279, Tallahassee, FL 32305-7886, USA, or www.dreamspinnerpress.
com.

Paperback ISBN: 978-1-64108-559-5
Digital ISBN: 978-1-64108-558-8
Paperback published April 2023
v. 1.0

Printed in the United States of America

"A single act of kindness throws out roots in all directions, and the roots spring up and make new trees." – Amelia Earhart

The author of numerous successful romance and romantic suspense novels, and a winner of RWA's Passionate Plume Award in 2011, **TERRY WYLIS** enjoys exploring the heart of a character, the depth of emotion that drives a person to exhilaration or despair, forming a bridge to the reader. Creating that depth is the first step to the fully-crafted works Terry loves to produce.

Terry strives to imbue her stories with kindness, allowing the reader to curl up with a cup of tea and escape the often harsh realities of the world. It may be one small act opening the door to a connection, or a character who adopts kindness as a lifestyle, but as Seneca taught, "Wherever there is a human being, there is an opportunity for a kindness."

At the same time, Terry is always "winding the watch of [her] wit; by and by it will strike" (William Shakespeare, *The Tempest*). The quick quip and witty repartee are her favorite forms of dialogue, and often a story idea will blossom from a single one-liner randomly gifted by her brain.

In addition to her literary pursuits, Terry enjoys poetry, crocheting, reading, New Orleans, all things British, forensics, psychology, and world cultures, along with whatever field happens to strike her fancy at the moment.

By Terry Wylis

DREAMSPUN BEYOND
Kissing Frogs

Published by DREAMSPINNER PRESS
www.dreamspinnerpress.com

Author's Note

I BEGAN writing this long before Covid came along, so this is an alternate universe.

For those who still believe in magic.

Acknowledgments

THANK you so much to the many brains who helped, whether with research points, beta reading, or simply keeping me sane: Aubrey, Damon, David, Ebs, Jo, Rob, Wendy, and WilMeij. Diamonds all.

Chapter One

HE was running out of time.

Certainly out of sanity. A year. One year, a hundred and twenty miles, icy water, biting wind, traveling any possible way he could, eating whatever he could find and then realizing his digestive system would no longer take just anything. That horrid, horrid moment when he realized exactly what he was going to have to do to survive. Learning to use the tools at his disposal before he starved. He'd thrown up every meal for a week before he finally got desensitized to the new diet.

At least he still had a fair bit of his strength. All things considered, his predicament could have been a lot worse. As long as he stayed away from the snakes. *Definitely* learned to stay away from the snakes. And the turtles. And the raccoons. And damn, the locals were grouchy. And loud.

He didn't speak the language. Anyone he found who *did* speak English either freaked out or threw him across the room. More than one had taken a shot at him.

Then that first winter. The drowsy terror as he watched the others sink beneath the water's surface, knowing he would have to do the same or freeze to death, not quite trusting the information he'd found that said this was the right decision. He was lucky to have gotten out of that internet café alive. The lady probably still hadn't stopped screaming.

God, people, get a grip already.

Eventually, overpowering sleep had solved his trust issues. And by some miracle the on-purpose "drowning" had worked. When he became aware of bright light and crawled out of the pond to warm sun and new grass, he thought for sure he'd died and gone to heaven. Until he looked down at his hands and realized nothing had changed.

Fuck it all, he couldn't even cry about it.

And now winter was coming again. He didn't even need to find a calendar or someone's phone this time. He could *feel* it. He had weeks, a month at the most. If he didn't find what he needed, he'd have to go back in the water, and he wasn't sure there'd be anything left of *him* when the sun came out again.

There wouldn't be anything left of Ellis Faraday.

THE broad profile of a turret rose into the afternoon sky, perfectly framed by two pin-straight rows of manicured evergreens flanking the walkway up to it. A

genuine turret, it and *two* others at the back visible from
the train station even with a river and a park between,
the one here at the front complete with diamond-paned
windows set in stone sills and an oxidized-green copper
roof, gray stone walls interspersed with Tudor-ish
sections of stucco and weathered timbers. It looked like
brick-shaped lights had been cemented into the sills
and the tops of the courtyard fence for subtle nighttime
illumination. Copper-colored gutters and downspouts.
Ruler-straight shingles with pointed finials on each
peak gave it even more dignity, and dormer windows
sidled out of the expanse to soften it away from being
truly forbidding. The only thing missing was a big-ass
double staircase spilling out of a second-floor foyer.
He got the distinct impression, for no reason he could
name, that at some point someone had compromised.

The whole thing crouched behind a huge circular
driveway-slash-parking lot designed for guests and a
smaller drive beyond for the owners. The circle's center
held a riot of summer flowers in their last fading throes,
interspersed with a few mums in reds, rusts, and golds. A
sumac at one end blazed with scarlet berries, reminding
him of his own mother's garden in late autumn.

Man. Fill that circle with horse-drawn carriages
and you'd be set for a production of *Cinderella.* Ellis
shook his head as much as he could. An actual fucking
castle sitting in a Massachusetts suburb.

Getting from the train station to the front gate had
been a nerve-wracking experience, between the cars
and the river. How the hell did others like him manage
to survive the few years he'd read about? They were
lucky to make it through any given twenty-four-hour
stretch without being eaten, squashed, poisoned, or
otherwise permanently maimed.

Anyway. Back to the fucking castle.

He could see generous woods at the edges of the property and assumed they probably carried on around back for an acre or two down to the river's edge. All tucked behind high stone walls and a wrought-iron gate. He noted the name *Townsend* carved into a brass plate, surrounded by more iron, sitting right in the center of that gate. An electronic keypad at the driver's side of it killed the whole medieval look, but 21st century and all.

Elegant, slightly aloof, but not *too* ostentatious. And he was an hour northeast of Providence, Rhode Island, not standing in front of some centuries-old Bavarian palace. There was only so much ostentatious they could manage.

Well.... The fact that he couldn't see anything gold-plated boded well for at least a decent helping of sanity. Could be the Townsends simply liked the mystery.

But clearly there was money. Which in America was about as close to royalty as he was going to get. Equally important, a spread this green in New England on October fifth meant an abundance of fresh water. And right now water meant food, shelter, and relative well-being.

He slipped through the gate and onto the cool grass surrounding the round driveway. Maybe, just maybe, he could find what he needed before winter came calling.

NOW *this* was more like it. Absolutely worth the ninja-level effort to get here. He hadn't seen an actual person yet, but sitting in the middle of a truly impressive stretch of lawn surrounded by woods was a pond. A small man-made one, about eight feet across, tidy and damn near perfect with its short stone wall and tall reeds along the back. A wooden lounge chair kept it company.

Behind him, the fucking castle was every bit still a castle. The turret at one end of the ground floor sported floor-to-ceiling windows along the entire wall, with exercise equipment visible within. The other rose from and almost bisected a hulking stone veranda that sheltered the ground floor and turned the second floor into private terrace space for at least two rooms. More stone on the ground floor formed a wider uncovered patio. What appeared to be a glassed-in lap pool cuddled up against the far side, and a detached stone shed completed the wide vista.

But the pond held his attention

Ellis moved closer for an inspection and found lily pads with a couple of pale orange flowers still clinging to the memory of summer. A small waterfall for circulation. Solar cells set into the stone shelf-border. Accent lights about a foot down would offer soft illumination after sunset. A gorgeous gazebo, the natural wood either varnished or polished to a warm glow, sat a short distance away.

And these two items felt... different. Even to his untrained eyes, none of it was built from a kit. Someone had put their heart and soul into this. Built with love.

Well, hopefully they'd be as passionate about helping a traveler in distress. And if they didn't help, at least he had a safe place to winter if he had to. A source of food, water, and shelter with minimal predators. It was enough. Hell, it was more than enough. He got comfortable and settled down to wait.

Chapter Two

"CAN you recommend a good book?"

Galen Townsend watched the very young lady's eyes widen as she looked up over the top of her reading glasses and then down over his body before she shook it off and smiled. "I'm sorry?"

Kinda ought to be after that, kid. Thought the whole #MeToo movement went both ways. The thought wasn't cool, and he silently apologized to the universe before settling a weary gaze on her. "Can you recommend a good book?" Lord, it wasn't rocket science. This was the city library, after all.

She glanced him up and down again and then stared at him as if he'd grown a third eye. "It's Friday night."

"Yeah. And?" Galen made a mental note to not discuss literature with anyone under twenty ever again.

Another once-over. "It's Friday night." She seemed to truly believe that explained everything. When he raised a brow, she blinked. "Um, shouldn't you be… you know, out?"

Okay, mental note to not discuss anything *with anyone under twenty ever again. Deploy Protocol Two: Sarcasm.* And maybe it would save her from pulling an eye muscle. Galen leaned his arm on the smooth granite top of the circulation desk and pulled up his best smartass grin. "Already there, sweetheart. Comfortably. For ten years now. And exactly what does my sex life and the fact that it's Friday night have to do with *whether you can recommend a good book?*"

She flushed bright red and pointed down the long main area. "Our staff picks are on the shelves just at the front of the fiction area, sir."

"Thank you." He turned away, shaking his head. *Why do I always get the idiots?*

"Hey, wiseass."

Her voice brought him back around, and this time the smile on her face was one that made his gut tighten in a not-nice anticipation.

"If you're so comfortable, how come you're here by yourself looking for something to read when everyone else is getting laid?"

Galen waited until she'd flounced off into one of the back areas before he let his spine relax and prayed his knees worked long enough to get the damn book and get home so he could be mortified in peace.

God, I hate teenagers.

"YOU'RE a disgrace to the Townsend name."

Not you too. Galen rolled his eyes as he tried to ignore his older brother primping in the mirror behind the wet bar in the parlor. "Reading, thanks." He settled further into the leather wing chair. The dark wood and brass sconces of the bar could have stood in for an Ivy-League version of *Cocktail* if Joe could mix a drink to save his life. Which he couldn't.

"I mean it. Here it is, Friday night. Boston's a mere hour away, teeming with lonely hearts just aching for the magic of the Townsend touch, and you're sitting on your ass with your nose in Emily Brontë." Joe's grin showed in his voice. "Not that that's such a bad thing, if she were still around. Might do you good to sample things this side of the river. Cure whatever's screwed up in your head."

The comment might have hurt, or pissed him off, if Galen hadn't long chalked up Joe's digs over his orientation to basic pain-in-the-assery rather than genuine prejudice.

"Now, Joseph, leave him be." The deeper tones of even older brother Ben filtered in from the formal entry. "You and I take care of half the set. He's got the other half all on his own. He's probably exhausted."

Galen sighed and looked up, slipping in the edge of the book jacket to mark his place. "Remind me again why Mom and Dad didn't leave the two of you out of their wills. And it's not Emily Brontë, it's John Grisham." He raised a brow and smirked. "Still want that visual, Joe?"

"Smartass." Joe finally decided every blond hair was perfectly in place and his tie was straight. "Come on, go get polished up and come with us. You know Storey McVeigh is dying to set you up with her brother, Treat."

"The McVeighs really hate their kids, don't they?" And clearly Storey had no clue that he and

Treat *had* gone out a couple of times, ending in a mutual decision of *yeah, no*. Galen went back to his book. "Are you planning to drag your conquests back to the cave, or am I okay to wander around the house naked all night?"

Joe snorted. "A Townsend doesn't need to drag, you know that. They come willingly. Hell, they beg for it. But the house is still Switzerland. Neutral territory. That's the whole reason we fork out for the condo in Back Bay." He picked up his suit coat from the polished walnut bar and shouldered into it. "You are officially hopeless, little brother. Come on, Ben." Several long strides, and the front door clicked with a bit more force than usual.

A gentle hand settled on Galen's shoulder. "You okay? I know he's a dick most of the time, but we both worry." Ben's blue eyes showed that concern when Galen looked up. "You could still come with us, you know. Just to get out for an evening. You never go to that club of yours anymore."

Galen shook his head and shrugged. "Waste of time. And I'm sick of the bouncer giving me the evil eye when he looks at my driver's license. I can't tell if he genuinely doesn't recognize me even after all this time or if he thinks the Vin Diesel routine counts as flirting."

Ben's deep chuckle filled the immediate space, even if it didn't reach the vaulted ceiling. "You'll get carded until you're fifty. Probably longer. Enjoy it. Some of us have to work to stay looking ten years younger than we are." The joke was no funnier now than the tenth time Ben had used it. Or the twentieth. A squeeze to Galen's shoulder. "Sure you won't come?"

"Yeah, I'm sure." The whole idea made him tired just thinking about it. "You guys go ahead. Schmooze the socialites and break a few hearts. I'm good."

A minute later he heard Joe's classic Audi squeal as it headed down the driveway. *Better take a look at it over the weekend. Might need to replace the brakes.*

Back to Grisham.

He lasted two pages before the silence of the house poked him one too many times. Galen sighed and got up, moving from the formal parlor to the generous and far less ornate kitchen/family room. He pulled a Corona from the fridge and settled on a stool at the big prep island.

He didn't even last a page.

The club didn't appeal. Like his brothers, Galen could walk into any club from Boston to Providence, gay or straight, and be holding court inside of ten minutes if he wanted. And he had, once upon a time. Bedding one of the Townsend boys was a fucking status symbol. The key to the kingdom, or so they all thought.

God, it was boring as hell.

If he wasn't gently breaking the hearts of ladies looking for more than dancing, he was reassuring some guy that yes, he really was twenty-seven even if he looked seventeen. No, he wasn't a twink or a model. And dear God, *no*, he didn't have a clue which body paint was all the rage for Pride Week. And he wasn't wearing ass-less Andrew Christian underwear or a ball stretcher, thanks much.

Maybe I'm the one who's boring. Read, work, build things, putter around on cars. In some small town in Ohio, that might be the in thing. Here in Attleboro, Massachusetts, not so much. The Townsend "kingdom" could be another country, as much as Galen felt connected to any of it.

He was tired of prowling, had been tired for a while now. It would be nice to find someone who could care less about the family fortune, who'd be every bit as happy curled up on the couch with nachos and beer and Netflix as they would showboating around the upper echelons of New England society. But he wasn't likely to find that person in the clubs.

The rate he was going, Galen figured it was about as likely as magic beans and golden geese he'd find them at all.

THE lawns at the back of the house, still velvet green even with autumn in full swing, stretched for a good acre before blending with the well-maintained woods making up the rest of the property. Inside the boundaries of the wooded section left wild, which stretched down to meet the Bungay River, nothing in the Townsend kingdom escaped being sculpted and managed to within an inch of its life. Soon the contracted landscapers would be aerating the lawns and giving the driveway trees a last trim before the snow flew. Still, there were times the attention to detail worked, creating pockets of beauty and relaxation.

Galen headed for his own little paradise, a gazebo and pond he'd built himself in high school, when the stresses of being gay in the shadow of the two most prolific playboys in eastern Massachusetts got to be stifling. Now the escape wasn't needed as much, but it was still a nice place—especially with twilight muting the sky in streaks of soft purple and blue and the first touch of generous crisp in the air signaling autumn's full settling in. He could breathe out here, think, plot, and generally goof off. With only the crickets to give him grief over it.

He set the book, his phone, and the Corona at the edge of the raised pond, a solid stone wall providing table space as well as the height for a small waterfall at the far end. He made a mental note to winterize the pump and plug in the heater sometime over the next couple of weeks. Solar lamps from the gazebo behind him provided enough light to read by. Galen settled into an Adirondack lounge and found his place again, finally losing himself in the world of legal intrigue.

"Now that is one fine setup you've got. The pond's nice too."

Interesting voice, light but cultured, with a rich undertone. It fit right in with the plot he was reading. Always great when he could hear the characters in his head.

"No fish. Kind of a bummer in terms of a meal. But then you'd probably be pretty attached to them anyway."

Wait.

Galen glanced over his shoulder, toward the gazebo. The teakwood structure with its plush seating was as empty as when he'd turned the lights on. He glanced around the pond area, squinting to see in the fading light down toward Ben's putting green a few yards away. *Maybe they came home early? But they just left.* Nothing but shadowed trees and soft grass, an owl hooting in the distance, the woeful call of a loon down on the river, the quick screeching bark of a fox.

"Down here, genius."

Down? He glanced over his shoulder again. The guys must have swung back around and were pranking him.

"Good God. On the lily pad. Next to the pretty orange flower. Excellent choice, by the way. Pink's way overdone."

What the hell? Galen glanced down at the water plants, shadowed heavily now. The voice did seem to be coming from that direction, but for the life of him he couldn't pick out the power light of a Bluetooth speaker. He got up and walked around the circumference of the pond, checking for a crouching figure. The border walls were high enough to hide Ben or Joe even now, though they'd have to be lying almost flat to the ground.

No one.

Irritated, mostly to avoid freaked-out, Galen sat back down on the lounge and reached for the beer bottle again. "Whoever you are, take a hike. Really not in the mood tonight. And you probably tripped the alarm around the perimeter, so the cops are on their way."

"Yeah, I'd love to see you explain that one." A squishy sort of *plop!* sounded right next to him on the pond wall. "Haven't tripped them yet, and I've been hanging around here for days waiting for someone to show up. Not like I've got the time to kill, with winter coming on fast. Don't you ever walk away from the Wii and *do* something?"

"I was in Hartford, troubleshooting for a client." Wait. Who the hell was he talking to? "Where are you?"

A prolonged and totally dramatic sigh. "Six inches from your *hand*, handsome. Right here."

"I think I'd notice you if— Shit!"

The beer hit the edge of his book, which hit the side of his phone, which took a swift and direct plunge into the pond and promptly sank.

"Well, that went well. Not." The frog that had startled him out of his mind hopped onto the arm of the Adirondack. "So, anyway. I'm looking for a princess. Or some sort of royalty. At least I think that's how this works. To break a spell. Kinda obvious, that, but I figure you're slightly freaked at the moment. Most folks are on first acquaintance."

Galen sucked in a breath and tried to get his brain back on track. Whoever was screwing with him had sure done it up properly, he'd give them that. Which meant it had to be Joe. He decided he might as well get his money's worth on it. He'd kick Joe's ass later. "You're under a spell. Right."

"And how many amphibians with a grasp of English do you know?" Or a grasp of dry snark, clearly. "I haven't found one yet, and I've been stuck like this for a year. By the way, let me give you some very smart advice right up front. Do *not* mess with magick users. Freaking scary when the warlock's got his shit together."

"Warlock?" Joe had outdone himself this time. Galen sat forward on the chair, narrowing his eyes and trying to pick out the trick.

"Yeah, go figure. And here I thought all the shiny rocks and weird bottles of stuff around his flat were just a serious Potter fixation. Who knew some of that shit's actually real?" Eyes the color of fresh 5W-30 motor oil studied Galen closely. "You're supposed to be a princess."

Oookay. He'd watched the frog's lipless mouth *move* with each word. Joe wasn't that good. A creepy little vibe started at Galen's tailbone and began crawling up his spine, along with the memory of an old children's tale his mother had read to him when she was still alive. He ignored the vibe and chose to salvage his sanity, sitting back and picking up the book again. "Wrong duck pond, friend."

The frog stared at him for a moment, and Galen could have sworn the hairless bump above one eye raised a fraction before the frog looked back and down into the pond. "I suppose you want your phone back. You'll be lucky if it's still working."

The memory of the children's tale provided a comeback. "Thought you chased golden balls." Galen purposefully opened his book, vowing to not speak to the pretty little hallucination again, even if it still sat at the edge of his peripheral vision. The stress was definitely starting to get to him.

"You got gold balls, dude? Wow. That's pretty cool. Gotta be hell on the sensation, though. That why you're here all by yourself on a Friday night?" Golden lidless eyes darted over the garden. "Are you sure there aren't any princesses around?"

Galen kept his eyes on the book and flipped a page. "Just me. And two pain-in-the-ass brothers. And family fortune aside, I am *not* princess material. I like my cars fast and my power tools organized. And my *men* hot." He renewed the not-speaking-to-the-hallucination vow.

"Hey, I'm hot. Or at least that's the going opinion. Seriously hot. Prior to the frogness. Possibly still. Haven't really asked around on that one."

Against his better judgment, Galen looked down again. Just a frog. He couldn't have named the particular species if he tried. About four inches long, bright green, dark circular spots with tan rings around them all over the back, sides, and legs. A thin pale stripe on each side trailing in parallel from the tops of those golden eyes to its butt, and another set framing its face. Sleek, slender, but athletic-looking. As frogs went, he supposed this one probably qualified as—

What the hell am I doing? He went back to reading. "Thought you were looking for a princess."

"I'm looking to not be a frog."

"Uh-huh. So you'll just take your kisses where you can get them, huh?"

"I always did that, sweetcheeks, even prior to the frogness."

Aside from the fact he was being addressed by an amphibian, Galen could appreciate the banter. Too bad the smart mouth came with teeny legs and a tendency to warts. Very bad in certain areas.

He gave up on the book. This conversation was entirely too weird to even pretend he could ignore it. He raised a brow at the frog and deployed the sarcasm again. "Well, seeing as you're probably right and the phone's fried, what's my incentive for kissing a slimy green shishkebab-wannabe with a mouth way too small to make me happy?"

Definitely a froggish not-eyebrow going up. "The chance I regain my hotness. And it would be a decent thing to do."

Damn, he hated it when the wildlife got logical on him. Galen glared at the little frog. "One kiss. And if I get warts on my lips, you're in big trouble. Got it?"

A four-toed foot raised in a clear defensive gesture. "Hey, man, just trying to get my mojo back. Not interested in anything else."

Figured. "God, I've heard that a thousand times…."

Gold eyes widened and the frog actually reared back slightly. "What sort of ponds have you been hanging out at? With those eyes and that tight form? Dude, seriously." A funny little snort, and he'd never imagined a frog could smirk. "Unless they all think you're jailbait. I'm assuming the Corona is legal and you only look like you're fifteen."

"Oh, shut up before I change my mind." Galen scooped up the frog, cradling it in his palm and staring into those golden eyes again. "You're actually *not* the worst thing I've ever kissed. Let's get this over with so I can make the insane decision to go to the club after all."

"Works for me." Could frogs grin? "And by the way, the whole warts thing is complete bullshit. But I'm not Frenching you on the first date."

"Ew. As if." He leaned down and brushed his lips over the frog's smooth nose. Cool, not nearly as slimy as he'd expected. Refreshing, sort of. He sat back, not sure if he expected something to happen or not. *Lord, I'm losing my grip on reality. Now I'm hoping frogs will turn into handsome princes. Note to self: Do not eat sushi at the Yakima Palace anymore. The chef is obviously having problems filleting the blowfish correctly.*

Whatever he expected, drugged up or not, it didn't happen. The frog just stared at him. Galen waited another minute, then sighed and got to his feet. "So much for that. Have fun." He tossed the frog back into the water and gathered up his book and the beer. *Maybe I'll just skip the club and go putter with the 'Vette all night.*

Chapter Three

SHIT, *shit, shit!* Ellis crawled back up onto the lily pad, wondering if he should simply beat his head against the stone wall of the pond and be done with it. Finally, *finally* he'd gotten a human to take him seriously, and the damn kiss didn't even work.

He'd assumed the huge house with its actual fucking turrets, high rooflines, and manicured lawns screaming "money" would work, providing he could get someone to listen to him. Would he have to find true royalty? America didn't have any; he'd have to get to a port and try to not get killed stowing away on a freighter to Europe where the rats were probably three times his size. It had taken him a year to get from New York City to here, barely the two-thirds point.

His family home was up in New Hampshire. Another hundred-plus miles.

There was no way. Not when the overnight temperatures were dipping into the fifties. It took forever to get moving in the mornings now; he could already feel the aching chill of evening seeping through him. According to the last internet search he'd managed—before people started freaking out over a frog on a table in a fucking café—he should be hibernating or getting ready to. He had at most, if the weather held, three weeks before he'd have to go into the water or freeze to death. A ship would have to wait until March or April, and by then he wasn't sure he'd have any sense of self left.

And it so figured, the single human who'd spoken to him without freaking out was pretty as well. Very pretty. Almost delicate features, but a strength in the jaw to offset. Slim build, lanky, a head of light brown hair with some curl to it, trimmed close enough even the longer top behaved. A prep-school look without the arrogance. Bright blue eyes, cheekbones high but soft, and lips full enough for a sexy little half-pout. Smart. And a smartass. God, that wit could dry out the Atlantic. Nice. The charm Ellis had once used at his own club scene just kicked in with this guy—whose name he hadn't even got, dammit.

Maybe he could try again in the morning. Especially if he retrieved Pretty Boy's phone from the bottom of the pond. It likely was completely fried, but if it was in one of those water-resistant cases.... Hell, worth a shot, and might net him a second kiss as thanks.

The water still held enough warmth at the surface to be navigable, and the single row of submerged lights gave him at least some illumination to go with the clear lid-ish membranes that allowed his eyes to focus underwater and protected them from debris, but he couldn't see the bottom of the pond. Hadn't been able to even at noon during the few days he'd been hanging around waiting for any sign of intelligent life. He could, however, measure depth by the number of kicks it took—something he'd worked out over the past year's experience.

Three feet… six… colder now, but not enough to slow him down. He resisted the instinct to inhale—*you can breathe through your skin, you can breathe through your skin*—the one thing he'd had to learn as a mantra because it just didn't compute to a human… brain, essence, soul, whatever it was now. The water was relatively clear, but there wasn't anything to see other than the faintly illuminated rock wall and a few drifting roots from the pond lilies and edge grasses.

At nine feet he started to feel the cold seeping in, the light faded completely, and the first notice of water pressure increase registered. *How the hell deep did they dig this thing?* He might have a foot to go, or another six. The cold blood in his frog veins made it increasingly difficult to move, to fight his own buoyancy. One last push, one last strain with eyes that hadn't evolved for miniature caving, and he gave up, letting himself float back up to the surface, crawling up onto the closest lily pad until he simply collapsed for a few moments.

Well, shit.

The disappointment crashed into him, weighing hard into depression, nearly sending him off the lily pad again. He crouched under the pond lily's petals, fortunately floating close enough to an accent light to pick up a little heat, and wished for the millionth time he could cry and release some of the pain. A strangled croaking moan was as far as he managed.

He stared into the light and let his mind empty of all thought. Better than useless pipe dreams.

HE must have fallen asleep, because he came very wide awake indeed when suddenly the lily pad was way too small and the pond still very deep and his fingers slid off the algae-slick driftwood log tucked into the reeds. The mantra went to hell as chill water closed over his head, poured up his nose and into his lungs. His legs felt like they weighed a ton and the muscles shrieked as he kicked out, kicked *up, up, goddamn it, up!* He grabbed for the edge and missed again, thrashed and kicked some more, and at last managed to hook his whole arm over the pond wall and find a protruding stone to grab on to. His entire being felt like overcooked spaghetti, with about as much strength, as he hauled himself bodily over the barrier and onto solid grass. He crawled up onto the lounge his host had been sitting in, coughing water from his lungs, snorting it out of his burning sinuses, willing himself to not scream at the same time. Only when he curled into a fetal position did the excruciating pain in his legs stop.

Wait.

His legs.

His arms.

He stretched his fingers out in front of him.

Oh my God.

Five fingers, not four. Pale skin, a little wrinkled from the water. No webbing. No freaky little pads at the tips. Fully visible from those tips to his wrist, and his neck *swiveled* to keep everything still in his sightline all the way up to his shoulder and down over his chest. The first time in a year he'd been able to see his own chest.

Am I dreaming? I don't feel like I'm dreaming.

He dared a glance down toward his feet. Human feet, still in his Amedeo Testonis, though the Italian shoes were shot to hell now.

Oh my God.

His breath backed up and he coughed his way through another few minutes.

It worked!

The elation took a rapid back seat when a gust of chill wind sent him into violent shivers and didn't completely die back to calm air. It was rising, and the humidity was fairly high as well. His suit and shirt were soaked clear through. He needed to get up to the main house before he froze to death. Hopefully the pretty man would let him use a phone. And possibly a shower.

He couldn't straighten his legs.

Too long. Too long as a frog, his legs compressed and compacted and bent whenever he wasn't hopping somewhere, and he couldn't get them into the right position for proper crawling, let alone walking upright, without another wave of agony. His gasp caught in his still-damp lungs, prompting another coughing fit, which just made his body hurt more.

I've got to find some kind of shelter. Eventually human flexibility would ease back, but the stretching would have to be slow and steady. He didn't have time. Another gust of wind seized his muscles and locked up his spine. He could barely move.

He shot a panicked glance around the darkened lawns, moonlit in the clear, cold air. *The gazebo!* It wasn't completely closed in, but there were benches and cushions and maybe a blanket or tarp he could use against the wind.

But first he had to get over to it. Certainly less distant than the main house, maybe twenty feet. But between the shivering, the muscle cramps, and the fact his spine was now in a completely different shape than it had been for a year, and a New England wind chill on top of that, he'd be lucky to get over to it before hypothermia literally stopped him cold.

Well, dammit, he hadn't hauled his itty-bitty frog ass almost two hundred miles only to give up in the last twenty feet at full size. He managed to slide out of the lounge and onto the grass, stopping to catch his breath from the searing pain in his thighs at even that much movement. God, he'd never complain about squats and leg presses at the gym again. He propped himself up on his forearms and pulled a few inches forward, lizard-like, his legs now spread in a poor imitation of his frog-crouch, making use of his hips more than his legs. At least the exertion would keep him warm for a few minutes.

By the time he pulled himself over the last step into the shelter of the gazebo, he was gasping, heart racing, muscles shuddering, throat dry, lungs burning clear down into their depths, body even wetter now with perspiration, and the wind had become a steady breeze rattling the wind chime hanging from a roof beam. He leaned his forehead on the smooth floor for a moment, willing the flashing sparkles in his vision to go away, for the vertigo to settle before he threw up all over the pretty rug.

Blanket... something.... There! Folded neatly in a wicker basket. Ellis managed to get his suit coat and shirt off before another wind gust seized his back up again for several moments. When that passed, he kicked off the shoes, crawled out of his trousers, and slithered over to the basket on his stomach.

Yes. *Oh dear God or whatever runs this planet, thank you.* Not one but two fleece blankets, full size, made for snuggling on the wide cushioned benches with another person. Ellis dragged them out flat as best he could, stacking them, then rolled onto them and up in them in only his boxers until he hit the solid bench base. He pulled the ends up over his head, curling back into his fetal position. The hard floor wasn't overly comfortable, but he'd never make it up onto the benches now, exhausted as he was. He was out of the wind, now blowing over the furniture barrier. Good enough.

He peeked out just enough to note the moon's position in the sky, though the stars were erased by the glare of the solar lights. A year of watching that moon had given him a fair sense of nighttime. It was around ten, give or take a quarter hour, and he estimated an hour or so had passed from his first panicked moments as a drowning human to now. He ducked back under the blankets and took stock. He had about eight hours to rest until someone at the house might be awake. By then hopefully he'd be able to at least crawl his way to the back patio and knock on a door. And then the nightmare would be over. He could go home.

The enormity of it all caught up like a punch to the gut and he curled tighter, chin dropping close to his chest. The tears he hadn't been able to cry for a year came out in torrents, making him shake harder, clogging his nasal passages and scraping his throat raw as he coughed out the last of the pond water.

Eventually, the exhaustion and emotional wringing took its toll and his eyes drifted closed. He'd figure out his next steps tomorrow.

A HEAVY... something... over his face left the air around him stale and sweaty. But his legs didn't hurt anymore. He offered another kudo to the universe for that.

Ellis's eyes registered faint light without the feeling of his eyelids rising—it felt like they *lowered* instead—and he realized the blankets felt much bigger, denser than he remembered from last night. But then he probably hadn't been particularly lucid, what with the cave-diving, the rock-bottom depression, the near-drowning, discovering he was human again, and then the mad rush for shelter and warmth. And probably was still exhausted. It would settle down eventually. He stretched, bracing for cold air on his feet as they cleared the blankets.

Nothing.

Wait.

His stomach gurgled. The few mosquito and beetle stragglers he'd found around the pond might have taken the edge off as a frog, but as a man again, he'd have to find something to eat fairly quickly or he'd pass out. His brain was already struggling to process his surroundings. He felt lighter, more... something... than he had last night.

He raised an arm to free himself from the blankets.

They barely moved.

What the...?

The light had intensified somewhat, and now he could stretch his hand out… but he couldn't see it. Or he could barely see it. Just the tips of his fingers.

Four fingers. Or more accurately, four *toes*.

Webbed toes.

Freaky little pads at the tips.

No.

He was dreaming. He remembered the desperate escape from the pond, the agonizing crawl to the gazebo. His suit and shoes would be a wrinkled pile on the wood floor. All of that was far too vivid still to have been a dream. So this was. He was just dreaming that he was a frog again, and it would go away as soon as the morning air hit him in the face.

Best get to it, then.

Finding his way out through the folds of fleece took him several minutes, following the light, nosing under layers where he could. He could feel the fabric leaching moisture from his skin.

I'm dreaming, I'm just dreaming, it's only a dream….

Cool air hit him in the face, the sky beginning to lighten, the wide lawns of the estate visible, the pond and the chair with the imposing house beyond. Ellis tried to turn his head and found himself still stuck in the dream, still a frog, and had to turn his whole body instead.

Yes, there were his sodden clothes. Muddy, grassy smears across the gazebo floor and on the steps.

So… it *had* worked? But why was he a frog again?

Dream looked less credible with every second. The cold morning air slowed him down, but the pond water had stayed warm enough near the accent light for him to get fully functional. The sun should be up in the next ten minutes or so and that would help further. He hopped down off the stone wall and onto the grass. Perfect timing as the sprinklers came on. More water misted over him and he felt his skin absorb it, suck it in like air. He felt less like a squeezed sponge and more like a frog, at least.

All right, all right. Take a breath and think, Ellis. Just think.

It *had* worked, temporarily at least. Probably because the guy's kiss had really been little more than a merciful peck on the nose. Ellis had no idea how long he'd stayed human, but it was only about six thirty-ish now, by the angle of the sun. Nor did he know for how long he'd given in to the near-hysterically-relieved tears last night, though he did recall calculating that he'd morphed to human at about 9:00 p.m. That would mean the spell had broken for... maybe three hours at the least? No, he'd probably feel far shittier right now if he'd been drying out under the blankets for a full six hours. Five hours human at the least, then, nine hours at the absolute most. The three was possible and he kept it in the back of his head, but it was probably a longshot.

So okay. All he had to do was find Pretty Boy again. Fortunately, the not-woods part of the estate wasn't that big. Ellis could see the back of the house, the wide veranda creating the second-floor terrace. And those two fucking turrets. Probably a hundred yards back to the courtyard by the front door and the third fucking turret. He *might* be able to figure out how to ring the doorbell; hell, he'd risk nose-butting the damn thing and giving himself a concussion if that's what it took. Or he could hang out and wait for Pretty Boy to emerge again.

It would take almost two hours for him to hop there, and hopefully the sprinklers had brought out the earthworms for a quick breakfast. Ellis had long since grown inured to eating insects, crawlies, and the odd minnow; he never had managed to get his stomach to adapt to anything much larger or... *ew*... covered in fur or feathers. With no teeny fish around—and better tasting than slugs—worms were his steak of choice.

Hopefully not for much longer.

Chapter Four

THE empty house at 8.00 a.m. on a Saturday didn't surprise him. Hell, he'd have been surprised if Ben and Joe *were* home. Galen poured a cup of coffee down in the kitchen, then moved back upstairs to his office space next to his bedroom, bare-chested and barefoot. He turned on his laptop in the small client area, letting it fire up while he checked his project board for the latest developments on their current dozen-or-so clients.

The Townsend brothers had taken the startup world by storm. If you had an idea, and if you could get past the front door, you'd just hired the A-Team.

Ben was the front door. With a Harvard Master of Finance and working on his doctorate, he had a knack for knowing exactly what sort of investment was needed for a specific business, from start to solid.

It might not agree with what the entrepreneur in his client chair *thought* they needed, but Ben's plans, if followed to the letter, never missed. He could—and had—turned many a washout into a blazing success simply by knowing when to inject a little more cash flow or when to pull it back and let the market handle itself. He also knew instinctively when an idea wasn't workable from the start, and wasn't shy about telling a potential client they might want to think in a different direction. He'd saved their clients as much money as he'd earned them.

Joseph was—no other word for it—a spin doctor. A marketing wizard with a gift for gab and a just-finished Yale master's under his belt, he could sell sand to the Saudis and make them believe they'd lived without it too long. Get a product or service on a solid footing, and Joe could make you the next Twitter.

Galen had never found much interest in finance or marketing. Or investment, for that matter. He liked getting his hands dirty, pulling things apart to see how they worked and putting them back together. He'd gone into mechanical and electrical engineering, a double bachelor's from UCONN with vague plans to add to it in the future, figuring he'd end up as a contractor or something while his brothers turned the world on its ear.

Then he'd found it wasn't so much the design he loved; it was troubleshooting. Finding the bits of a manufacturing plan or prototype that didn't work, figuring out *why* it didn't work, and puzzling out how to *make* it work.

It was a perfect match. If one of their clients hit a production snag, Galen was boots on the ground, toolbelt and tablet in hand.

In five years they'd taken their combined inheritance and turned it into something properly huge, and brought a lot of folks along with them.

Not much for him on the board this morning, mostly stuff for his brothers. Things he should be aware of but that didn't directly involve him yet. He did need to follow up on two field visits, and a motor should be arriving from Seattle in today's FedEx. A trip to Canton, Ohio, week after next for ProCircuit. After he ate breakfast and got through a shower, it would all be waiting for him. He pulled the files he needed from the cabinet and laid them on his worktable in the bigger space at the north end of the room, glancing out the window overlooking the back lawns on his way past.

That was so weird. Maybe he'd actually dozed off and just dreamed he'd gone down to the pond last night? But he couldn't remember going directly from the parlor conversation with his brothers to his bedroom. He decided to retrace what he could remember, starting back in the kitchen. Yes, there was a Corona bottle in the recycling bin, and he knew that Molly, their part-time housekeeper for as long as he could remember, had emptied it before she left Wednesday afternoon. A quick glance into the garage showed his tools put away but a couple of stained shop rags on the workbench. So he hadn't dreamed working on his car, either.

And his phone wasn't in his bedroom, his office, or on the communal charging station in the downstairs hallway. He was moderately obsessed about knowing where his phone was, since it was a business lifeline; if it wasn't in one of those three spots, it was essentially nowhere to be found.

So what the hell was that? Frogs didn't talk. They didn't trade quips with him, they didn't proposition him, and they sure as hell didn't turn into princes. Maybe he should make an appointment for another physical. Did an aneurysm do shit like this to your brain?

He'd made it through eggs and toast, cleaned up the dishes—and ordered a new phone with express delivery via the business landline in Joe's office—when the video doorbell at the gate rang.

As expected, FedEx. Galen punched the latch release and shrugged into the T-shirt he'd left on one of the breakfast-bar stools while the driver brought the package up to the door and knocked once to let Galen know it was there before heading back to her truck. Standing instructions on their account they'd used for years.

"There's that, then." The box from Gyro Systems, noted to his attention on the label. Going over the specs for it should take up most of his morning. Joe and Ben would drag themselves home by noon at the latest. He bent to pick up the box.

"Bedhead's a decent look on you, Galen Townsend of Townsend Consulting, LLC. Not everybody can pull that off."

No. Not again. Coming from the tall plant pot to his left, so probably read the address label on the box. God, he needed to call Dr. Orulu today.

"Mind if I come in? We've got a bit of a problem."

Don't look, don't look, don't look....

Galen turned his head.

Fresh-oil eyes, bright green skin, leopard-like spots, pale stripes, a pearly green-white belly now visible. Frog legs. Frog face. His voice scrunched itself up into a strangled whisper as he leaned his forehead on the box. "I'm crazy. That's it. I'm crazy. They're going to lock me in a padded cell...."

"Well, the white coats aren't here yet, so maybe we ought to get that box inside before you screw up your back completely or I nearly drown again." Gentle amusement from the amphibian as a soft thump vibrated through the box and into Galen's skull. "You're cute in that position, but you really shouldn't tease."

Okay, the propositioning sounded familiar, at least. And playing along felt infinitely better at this point than trying to fight it, so Galen simply picked up the box-with-frog and headed back up to his office.

He set it on his desk and checked to see if he was still hallucinating. Yep, there sat the frog, staring at him, an amazingly obvious raised brow going on for a face that had no eyebrows— or discernable eyelids, for that matter. He lasted about ten seconds under that unblinking *Well?* expression. "So... you... said we had a problem?"

"Yeah. Like maybe the fact that I ruined my favorite suit and a pair of Amedco Testonis by waking up on a seven-inch lily pad at six foot two." Damn, frogs had a hell of a glare. And apparently *did* blink on occasion, though it looked really weird going from the bottom up. "I thought I was never going to make it out of that hole. Felt like my quads were ripping in two every time I kicked."

"Wait. You mean it worked? My kiss worked?" He really shouldn't give in to insanity, but it was getting pretty hard to ignore. A smile started to curve his lips before he caught it. "That's an ego boost, thanks."

The frog wasn't amused. "Dude, I almost drowned! Who the hell digs an eight-foot koi pond over nine feet deep?"

Galen felt his ears heat. "Uh, I had way too much fun with the Bobcat from the rental place? I was fourteen."

For some reason he could picture a human eyeroll to go with that little snort. "Yeah, I can see that happening, just from last night and this morning." The frog squirmed. "By the way, would you mind if I took a dip in the bathroom sink? I keep forgetting this whole *not outside, skin dries out, I feel like shit* thing."

"Yeah, sure." It really did feel much better to simply go with the insanity. He picked up the frog and opted to go back down to the kitchen instead. The rear stairs railing kept him marginally connected to reality. "Uh, anything else you need?"

"Wouldn't say no to an earthworm or two. Pickings were a little slim under the sprinklers. It's getting too cold for them."

Okay, since he was fairly sure he hadn't known that particular science fact before now, hallucination theory was stretching a little thin. But it still felt better to his brain than—

"Galen."

His attention snapped back to the present. "Huh?"

"Wa-ter. Please. Preferably before I desiccate."

Oh. "Sorry." He filled one side of the sink with a couple inches of water from the tap. "Here you go."

"'Scuse the lack of style. Belly flop's all I've got at the moment." A rather large *plop!* left Galen reaching for a towel. The frog heaved an enormous sigh and a gravelly little groan. "Oh shit, that's better, even if it's city water. I'd have been home ages ago if it wasn't for the fact that public transit is remarkably low on open water sources or, you know, dew or moist soil. One of the reasons I got off here, aside from the whole

Oh my God, there's a for-real castle across the street thing. That pretty little river between you and the train station." Another groan-y sigh. "So, what's for breakfast?"

"You mean besides you on a skewer over my grill?" The rapid back-and-forth between serious and sarcasm couldn't be healthy, but the frog seemed to bring out the brat in him.

"Uh, yeah, not into the whole BDSM thing, thanks. And you are such a grouch when you aren't getting any."

Case in point.

"Where's home?" Galen rummaged through the refrigerator, thinking hard. What did frogs eat? Fish, maybe? Problem was, Joe did most of the everyday cooking in the family, unless Ben was on a tear, and as he didn't like fish.... Galen moved to the pantry.

"New Hampshire. Family estate on Massabesic Lake. Land's been ours for, oh, about three hundred years now."

Okay. He'd asked. A completely insane answer matched everything else so far. "Uh, I think Joe got a can of sardines from a client, like months ago." He opened a couple more cupboards before he found it. "Water packed and no salt. Those work?"

"I'll take it."

While the frog ate, Galen poured another cup of coffee for himself, then sat down at the kitchen island and rested his head in his hands. *Was* this what going nuts felt like?

He must have dozed off or zoned out from the stress, because the next sound he heard was his brother's voice.

"Galen!" Ben strolled into the kitchen, managing to still look polished in his slightly rumpled suit, his hair obviously well-fingered from whoever he'd spent the night with. "Hey, buddy, remember the Switzerland rule you were giving Joe hell about last night? What gives?"

"Huh?" Galen glanced around the kitchen. The sardine plate was empty, but the frog was nowhere to be seen. "I didn't have anybody over, Ben. What are you talking about?"

"Uh, *this*?" Ben held up a pile of wet clothing in one hand and a pair of really trashed dress shoes in the other. "Found them in the gazebo—along with a mess of blankets, mud, and grass, mind you—when I went out back for a little early putting." He laid the items on the kitchen island. "I know they're not yours. You hate Italian shoes."

"Okay, so your fashion sense sucks. I suppose I can live with that." The now-familiar voice came softly from the direction of Galen's coffee mug, still half full and cold now. He glanced down and saw the dishtowel he'd left there after his minor sink-shower move slightly.

Ben apparently hadn't heard, or registered, the exchange. He was checking out the suit coat. "Hmm. Custom-made. Ellis Faraday... can't tell if that's the owner or the designer."

A snort came from under the dishtowel. "If this transformation thing works again tonight, I am so kicking his ass for that."

Owner, apparently. Galen now had a name to put with the voice. Ellis.

"So A, whose are they, and B, why the hell are they muddy and soaked?"

"Uhh…." How the fuck was he going to explain this, especially when he'd just been smacked in the face with solid proof he *wasn't* hallucinating and the frog's insane story was real?

The chirp of Ben's phone saved Galen from having to come up with an excuse. His brother's brain shifted to business as he laid the jacket back onto the pile. "It's Davis. I gotta take this before he decides it's really okay to dump eighty percent of his operating budget into home shopping ads. Just… clean up after your guests, huh, Galen…." He disappeared off toward the end of the house containing his bedroom and office.

"Yeah, sure. Sorry about that." Galen waited until he heard the door to Ben's office close. "Wow, that was close."

The frog crawled out from under the dish towel. "I've always had excellent karma. Well, except for the one kinda obvious…."

"So Ellis is your designer, huh?" A smirk seemed fitting for the moment.

The frog fixed a perfectly readable *go-to-hell* look on him. "Smartass. Could we maybe find your computer?"

"Sure." He was halfway up the back stairs again before he realized. He turned and shrugged. "Sorry."

"Not an invalid, but thanks. At least you gave me a view to behold on your way out." Ellis hopped from the counter to a stool and then to the floor. Pretty decent stride for a creature less than six inches long, and Galen smiled as he said so.

"Yeah, I figure my quads are gonna be ripped once I get out of this mess and can get them properly straightened out again. I will be utterly kickass on the bike trails." Ellis caught up with him. "So, let's go find a spot to chill and I'll tell you the long version."

"I AM a prince. Or the next best thing to it here in the States. Ask anybody." The frog tried to hop up onto Galen's desk stool in vain. After three more attempts, an exasperated glare hit Galen from ankle height. "You going to just stand there and wait for me to keel over from a coronary, or could I persuade you to lend a hand here?"

"You made it down from the kitchen counter and up the stairs." Galen was reasonably sure he'd heard that grunt/growl response on a television show some years back, one that translated nicely to *I will hurt you.*

It still didn't completely erase the feeling of being on one of those hidden-camera shows. Or possibly still dreaming. And he hadn't quite given up on the blowfish theory, either. *Things like this do not happen in real life.*

"*Down*, sport. Operative word there. Gra-vi-ty. And the stairs are only eight inches high, not three feet. Which is the outer end of my vertical limit, by the way. What is it with you and stools, anyway? Isn't there a regular chair anywhere in this house?"

"Better on my back when I'm working." Galen reached down and lifted the frog up to the seat of the chair, watching it hop the rest of the way onto the desk and over to his laptop. *This is insane.* "What are you trying to do?"

"Duh. Prove to you what I've been trying to say for the last twelve hours." A hand—*Paw? Foot?*—no bigger across than Galen's pinky fingertip punched at a button. "Though, the rate I type at the moment, it's going to take another three to find what I need to."

Maybe Joe drugged my Coke at dinner last night. Galen pulled out the stool and sat down. "Okay, what am I searching?"

"Ellis Roland Faraday. The Third."

Galen started typing, his inner brat kicking in again. "Do I get to call you Rollie?"

"Do and I'll find one of those not-yet-hibernating earthworms and drop it down your throat while you're asleep." Ellis pointed a teeny foot at the screen. "Right there at the top. That's me."

Faraday Heir Missing. No Leads. The link led to a local New Hampshire newspaper website, the article dated thirteen months back. "How come this wasn't national news?"

"We're not that sort of American royalty. More a historical legacy than financial. Don't get me wrong, we're not living in a log cabin or anything, but Dad made his money in logging and fishery before he switched over to renewables when the timing was right. Hardly a shark in the Wall Street waters. Never one to get too attached to his portfolio."

Galen checked a couple more articles. "Says here they had a suspect, but he wasn't making any sense. Passed a polygraph with what they're calling a fantasy story."

Another hearty frog-snort. "Knowing Wayne, he told them exactly what he did. But 'I turned my date into a frog during a long weekend in New York' doesn't tend to reassure law enforcement in small towns. Though it might fly in Los Angeles."

Galen realized he'd just had thirty seconds of conversation with a frog *without* thinking *this is nuts* even once. Curious, he clicked on the browser's Images tab. *Wow*. School portraits, candid shots, a selfie or two… and all the same. Tall, lean, with legs that went on forever. Platinum blond hair falling straight over and around an oval face and light green eyes. A wide, sensual mouth that looked every bit as inviting in a reserved smile as it did at full wattage.

"Yep, that's me. Unfortunately, a platonic kiss in the name of fair trade wasn't enough. Far as I can tell, from the moon position after I finally got out of that pond and somewhere I wasn't going to freeze to death, I was human from about 9:00 p.m. to anywhere between midnight and six in the morning. Didn't notice when I changed back. I was pretty wiped out. Sucks to be me."

"You can tell time by the position of the moon?" Better that than imagining the man in the photos lying mostly naked in the gazebo. "Okay, impressed."

"Been a frog for over a year, man. You pick stuff up."

The banter felt better and less insane by the minute. He'd always liked guys who could match him quip for quip. Galen raised a brow. "So you're stuck as a frog except for three to nine hours a night? Until what?" He smirked. "True love's kiss, right?"

"God, I hope not." Ellis's small frog body shuddered. "That'll take forever. I'd settle for a decent interlude in the sack."

Galen wasn't going to imagine that yet, either.

THE morning passed fairly quickly. While Galen started his diagnostic pass on the motor, Ellis filled him in on the whole story. Wow. A year. Alone. As a frog, and a small one at that. Sounded like one of those fancy

BBC nature shows with the custom cameras. Only Ellis hadn't had a backup crew.

Rather than walk back and forth to a sink every hour, they'd solved the water issue with a deep baking dish and a couple quarts of pond water, decked out with an overturned bowl so Ellis could catch some warmth from the sun coming in the windows when he wasn't soaking.

When they took a break, Galen figured if he was going to have a guest for a few days at least, a little basic zoology was in order. "Do you know what species of frog you got turned into?"

"Actually, yeah." Ellis kicked once and covered the length of the baking dish, then shifted back the other way. "I got lucky the second day, after a complete freakout and getting the hell away from Wayne the Warlock. He lives half a block from Central Park, the only obvious fresh water source that's not an imminent health hazard. Stopped to catch my breath. Little girl fascinated by wildlife, thanks to some Brit naturalist on YouTube, and a fucking awesome dad armed with one of those identifier phone apps. I am a northern leopard frog." He crawled up onto the bowl and stretched out one back leg, then the other, giving Galen a bizarre mental flash of a frog yoga class. "One of the very few times interacting with humans ended well. They put off catching the subway so they could sit on a bench by that lake and learn stuff. My hanging out with them for twenty minutes or so was mutually educational."

Galen brought Ellis back to his desk computer, punched "northern leopard frog" into the browser, and was rewarded with several articles and a video of frog calls. He clicked on the video link and listened before trying to stifle a laugh. "They *snore* at each other."

Another few seconds and he lost the battle entirely. "Oh my God, they *snore* and they *giggle*." He managed to pull back most of his own laughter before he glanced at Ellis. "Can you do that?"

Another go-to-hell glare. "Earthworm, sport. Wiggling around inside your sleeping mouth. I know where the biggest ones hang out on your lot. I will *not* rinse it off first."

"Okay, okay, sorry." Galen lost one more snort of laughter before he got it under control. "Seriously, though, can you make those sounds?"

Ellis sighed. "Wayne apparently wasn't up on the particulars. I got stuck with my own vocal cords in the frog body. Helpful for communicating with humans, not so much for sounding like a real frog. I suck at it. Tried half a one for the kid, since I didn't want to scare her to death, and managed about a quarter. I think they figured I was afraid of them and didn't seem concerned by the lack of a serenade. When they turned to go, I hitched a ride to the subway in the bucket she'd been using to play in the water and collect interesting rocks. Got out of the bucket and under the seat before she noticed. Cute kid. And by the way, subway cars should be listed as EPA hazard zones."

"That's an amazing story." Galen checked for a couple of basic information sheets and printed them off before moving back to his worktable and reorienting himself to the diagnostic. He'd read them once work was done.

Ellis waited a few minutes until Galen was back on track before he spoke again. "So how come you were out by the pond on a Friday night anyway? I'd think by now the club bouncers would have seen your driver's license enough to not hassle you."

Galen reached for a larger screwdriver from the tool cart behind him. "Sick of the clubs. Have been for a while. Ben and Joe still like the whole Townsend-playboy thing, but I guess I'm lazy or something. It's too much work for a one-night stand." And wasn't it weird his deepest secret tumbled right off his lips to a near-total stranger.

"Or you want someone to stick around for more than one night. I get it. Someone who likes you when you're just kicking back doing your own thing. Talk books, work on the car, build stuff…." Ellis paused long enough that Galen looked up, and sure enough, those browless eyes did a great imitation of eyebrows waggling. "Spend all day in various erotic and possibly gymnastic endeavors."

Dammit, he never had outgrown the epic blush. Galen felt it flare from the tips of his ears clear down to his navel. The frog's not-frogish chuckle didn't help at all.

"Got you thinking, didn't I?" Ellis left his makeshift pond and hopped over next to Galen's tools. "God, that's a pretty blush. Wanna try another kiss?"

"Or I could wait until nine tonight and kiss you for real." His mind—ignoring the whole *total stranger* thing again—had wandered right into those images anyway, tangling his fingers in pale strands and pulling that long body close to his….

"But what if it doesn't work that way? What if I don't change back tonight?" No banter this time. That was pure plea. "Galen, I don't want to go through another winter like this. I don't think I *can*. I—"

The plea cut through to the center of his gut, along with a new sensation of the sheer loneliness Ellis must have felt. "What?" Galen set down his tools and gave Ellis his full attention. "What do you mean by that?"

Ellis had gone back to his mini-pond and was sitting in the shallows by the bowl. "Nothing. It's not going to work if it's out of pity. Just forget it."

The change in mood struck Galen more than anything. *He needs a friend. Maybe so do I.* Whether anything more happened or not. He picked up the frog, resting his elbow on the desk so they essentially sat eye-to-eye. "The first one was more or less out of pity, and it netted you a few hours. Come on, tell me. Please."

A ripple of muscle along one side in an approximation of a shrug, but Ellis's gaze seemed to be focused over Galen's shoulder. "It's not just getting home. I need to be *me* again. I can feel that slipping away. Weeks and months of nobody to talk to, stuck in my own head in a world where I don't speak Frogish, where I can't read the signals, where the ones I do know only work on humans who either run screaming or try to kill me." Ellis finally shifted to look directly at him. "Finding you helps. It's a connection. But I'm still losing me. And I'm afraid—hell, I'll admit it, I'm fucking terrified—that if I go into hibernation one more winter, there won't be anything left of *me* when I wake up. Nothing left but a frog."

"That's not going to happen. We'll figure this out." Damned if he didn't believe it. Galen brought his hand in and pressed a gentle kiss to the frog's back. "We'll figure it out. I promise." He set Ellis back on the desk. "Now, I need to get this done. You want to sit here and watch me, or is there a show you're dying to catch up on?"

Those fresh-oil eyes widened perceptibly and two browless eye bumps twitched. "*Game of Thrones* on Netflix?"

Galen looked into that hopeful froggy gaze and couldn't decide if he should warn the little guy or not.

HE should have been watching the show. He'd been obsessed with the medieval drama. Now, though, Ellis found his attention wandering back to his new friend.

Galen's focus was all for the small motor in front of him, tool kit on one side and tablet on the other. He'd loosen a bolt, set it aside, make a sketching motion on the tablet... then go back for more. Over and over and over, clearly building a detailed schematic in two minute increments. A clean sheet of paper waited on the drafting table behind him to become a larger hard copy. When something was obviously out of place, Galen's thin brows would curl together and a soft little snort would fluff the air around him. Notes got scribbled, then he'd dig in a drawer or dash out of the room and come back with a different part. More scribbles. More little snorts and bemused headshakes. A couple of eyerolls. Dear God, it was adorable. The passion and love for his work showed plainly on Galen's face.

When had *he* ever been that passionate about something? Ellis had barely decided to get his own life in order when Warlock Wayne shot his life to hell. He'd had some ideas, yeah, but nothing had really grabbed him. Not like *this*.

"Bored already?"

"Huh?" Ellis realized he'd been staring, and now Galen was staring back at him.

"I get like that when I haven't watched a show in a while. Takes time to get into it again. I can back it up to last season if you want." Galen glanced at the clock. "Oh wow, I didn't realize I've been sitting here all afternoon. I get into a project and the world sort of goes away, you know? Sorry about that."

"No, no, it's fine." Damn good thing frogs didn't blush or he'd look like a mutant tomato about now. And if Galen was right about the clock, Ellis had spent most of those same five hours staring at Galen while the show binged itself. "You love what you do. It shows."

"I get a chance to dig in like this with about a third of our clients. Rest of the time they either get stuck at the money end and Ben's the one unraveling a knot, or it all goes off without a hitch and it's up to Joe to sell it." Galen stretched his arms up over his head and leaned back over the drafting stool. "You hungry? I think we skipped lunch."

"Could eat. I—" Ellis ducked into his mini-pond as a new person strode into the office.

"Hey, bro." Longer and lankier than Galen or Ben, lighter in both hair and eyes, coiled energy in every step, Ellis suspected Joe Townsend could own any room in ten seconds flat if he chose. The killer grin would manage it in five at close range.

Galen, apparently long immune, continued tidying up his work area and his files. "Joseph. When'd you manage to drag yourself home?"

"'Bout two. Running a little late on account of *Mona*." The simple name gained three syllables. "Not like I had much for me on the board that can't wait till Monday." Joe gave the motor on the desk a once-over from about three inches distance. "This Gyro Systems? What's the lowdown, Mr. Wizard?"

Ellis started to crawl over the edge of his pond, wanting to get a better look at the newcomer, but suddenly a book nearly gave him a concussion as it settled on top of the baking dish. He hadn't even seen Galen come this way.

"They just need bigger circuit breakers. Too much power going through these, they pop before the motor can even start. Whoever they've got for an engineer needs a refresher or something. I tinkered with this model and tablet-sketched new schematics for them. I'll email them a report tomorrow and FedEx them a full-sized blueprint by Monday." Galen stayed right next to him, and from the shadow of his arm through the thick glass Ellis could tell a slim hand rested on top of the book. A warning: *stay put and stay hidden.*

"Cool. Already got some ad ideas percolating." Joe paced the length of the desk once more. "Ben says come eat. He whipped up his Thai Chicken, and I was nice and brought home sushi for you mutants since I was coming past Zen Crab anyway. And you're not gonna believe this. That fishing guy... Perkins... mailed me a freaking case of those sardines. I've told him six times already I don't do fish." A verbal shudder followed that statement.

"Be right there." As soon as Joe cleared the doorway, Galen picked up the book and set it back on the end table by the generous sofa. "Sorry about that. Joe's got a thing with fish, frogs, and just about anything else semi-aquatic. You'd think he'd have outgrown it by now, but... I just saved you from another one of those throw-you-across-the-room deals."

Ah. "Much appreciated. So, I'm thinking bad idea to join you at the dinner table." He shouldn't feel hurt by that; they'd already had plenty of time to themselves and likely would have more after dinner. But it still stung a little. Ellis shrugged it off as best he could in his current form. "No big. I can keep on bingeing." Or back the remote up and start over, since he'd paid no attention whatsoever to the television all afternoon.

"I won't be long. They'll both have plans for tonight as well. I'll bring you back a plate of sardines." Galen picked him up and trailed a finger down his back. Shit, that felt good! "We'll curl up in my room and find something decent to watch."

Ellis suspected he'd pay about as much attention to the television as he had so far today. "Sounds like a plan."

Chapter Five

GALEN stirred, shifting his arm up over his head onto the pillow, slipping further into the dream.

Morning cast his bedroom in a golden glow, bright even through his mostly closed eyelids. Long, gentle fingers trailed up over his chest, tickling his armpit, making him shiver as the touch continued down his arm until those fingers twined with his.

"Hey."

"Hey yourself." He turned his head toward Ellis, opening his eyes fully, drinking in the light green gaze with the blond strands falling into it, the soft smile. God, what a way to wake up.

The other adventurous hand headed down over his stomach, his hip, his thigh....

"Galen?"

"Hmm?" He let his eyes drift closed again as Ellis pressed kisses to his shoulder, that lean touch on a return trip up his inner thigh, the room going dark as he focused on nothing except his lover's touch and the heat curling low in his gut. "Oh shit, that's good...."

"Galen?" A pause, and that smooth tenor vibrated against the edge of his ear. "Are you cheating on me already, bro? Thought you were saving those gold balls just for me." A very *cold* set of fingers settled over his arm and squeezed.

Galen came fully awake with a gasp, nearly falling out of the big bed as he scrambled away from the dark figure barely edged in the moonlight coming in through the curtains. "What? Who? Fuck!" He got hold of the lacrosse stick mounted on the wall above his bed. "Get the hell out of my bed, you perv—"

Wait.

A light brow, barely visible in the dim light, raised slowly over a very white smile. "You invited me into your bed, sport. Remember? Set up a towel on the plastic wrap so's not to soak your pillow? I moved it, by the way. Figured you didn't want to have to take a blow dryer to the mattress."

"I—" He kept his grip on the makeshift weapon and reached for the bedside light switch.

Pale green eyes, white-blond strands falling over them, soft smile, the lanky form from the web photos stretched out on his bed... wearing nothing but wrinkled boxers.

Galen fought to draw a breath and sank back onto the bed. "*Ellis?*"

"Yeah. Nine on the dot. You dozed off about halfway through the movie." Long fingers removed the lacrosse stick from his grip and set it back in its hooks before returning to smooth the hair over Galen's ear. "That's at least partly my fault. I'm sorry I've been a bit of a strain on your sanity."

Galen watched a shiver run through Ellis's body. Then another and another. His brain finally kicked in. "God, you must be freezing. Let me at least get you a T-shirt." Thank God his brothers were occupied elsewhere tonight; his freakout would have had them both stampeding into his room.

He started to get up, but Ellis caught him by the hand. Galen stopped. "What?"

"Rather have you warm me up. The shirt can wait." That pale green gaze pleaded with him. "Frogs don't cuddle, and they all figured out real quick during breeding season that something was weird about me, thank God." Ellis shuddered again, but Galen didn't read it as a cold-shiver this time. "Frog sex is some seriously messed-up shit, by the way. But I haven't touched or been touched by anyone, human or critter, in over a year. Well, unless there was someone's potential dinner involved, or a wall." Long fingers tightened around his. "Not looking for anything more than another body in close proximity. That's all. Little early for anything more anyway."

"Yeah, sure." Galen lifted the covers and let Ellis situate himself before crawling back in next to him. He couldn't quite work out if he was disappointed or not that Ellis had made it very clear this was only for warmth; hell, for all he knew, he was still dreaming.

Ellis moved close, shivers still wracking him. Galen pulled the slim form tight, rubbing cold limbs, noting Ellis still had his legs bent almost to fetal position. Oh. "You need some help getting your legs to stretch out again?"

"In a minute. When I can actually feel my toes." Ellis sighed, his head on Galen's shoulder. "Liking this."

"Me too." It was nice. He'd never taken the time to just cuddle with someone like this, before or after anything more. Or if he had, it hadn't been like this. Lazy. Quiet. And should it feel damn near perfect when they barely knew each other? He felt Ellis's skin start to warm, felt the shivers relax. The blond strands between his fingers felt better than he'd daydreamed.

When Ellis snuggled closer and his feet against Galen's calves no longer felt like icicles, Galen eased up and tucked the blankets around Ellis, smiling at the protest. "I'm going to get you a sweatshirt and a pair of socks so you'll stay warm while we work on those quads. That's all."

A little lopsided pout accompanied a groan. "Cuddle me and then torture me. I see how this is going to work."

"Well, I can't feel good about cuddling you when I know you're still a pretzel." Galen returned to Ellis's side of the bed, pressing a kiss to a high forehead. Perfectly natural to do that, it seemed, at least according to his subconscious; he hadn't even thought about it. "Come on, let's get the torture part over with." He lifted the blankets just enough to slip the warm wool socks he used for hiking onto narrow feet, then eased the heavy UCONN sweatshirt over Ellis's head, hearing sounds of discomfort in even the act of sitting up slightly. "Sounds like your back isn't happy, either."

"Nothing's happy." The pout was back, along with pleading eyes. "Can't we just skip it tonight? I'll be a frog again at some point before sunrise."

"You don't know that for sure." Galen began to rub one of Ellis's long thighs, gently easing it straight in tiny steps, offering soft sympathy and encouragement.

It took a full hour. The other took a further hour.

And Ellis was clearly in pain all through it, though he said nothing and simply dug into the sheets until his knuckles were white. Galen spoke gently about everything and nothing, doing his damnedest to provide any sort of distraction.

Finally Ellis sighed and lifted Galen's hand away from its work, pressing a kiss to Galen's palm. "You're going to be dragging tomorrow. And you'll be lucky if you can hold the pen to your tablet. But God, that feels so good." He glanced at the clock. "Wow. Okay. So, nine to at least 1:00 a.m."

"Let's see if we can improve on that, since now I don't feel like I'm fondling an invalid." Or a *complete* stranger. Galen let his fingers trail up Ellis's strong jawline to tangle in platinum strands. "I've been dreaming about kissing you properly since I saw your photos."

The lean body relaxing further was prize enough, but the soft moan and the movement of Ellis's mouth against his left Galen dizzy. Eager fingers played in his hair, over the curve of his ears, and under his jaw. Galen traced kisses over high cheekbones, long lashes, and curved brows before returning to the generous mouth and soft lips. His body stirred, but he kept things slow, pulling back gently when Ellis tried to probe with his tongue. "Easy. Let's take it easy. I don't want this to be just a romp in the sack. You're the first person in a long time who wasn't just an attraction. You feel like a friend." He grinned. "For the moment, at least."

Long fingers tightened over the back of his neck, and the verdant gaze pleaded again. "This has to work, Galen. It has to. I can't—"

"Shh." He savored Ellis's mouth again for long seconds. "We have some time. You said something about a couple weeks?"

"I think so." Ellis toyed with the hem of Galen's shirt. "Last year it came on sort of like a cold. A weird, drowsy fog in my head. I couldn't get warm because the sun was lower in the sky. I can feel it starting to happen again, even now. The first touches of it. A frog instinct, I guess. Like when a sound hits that one little nerve in the back of your brain, you know?"

"Yeah." Galen chuckled. "Happens a lot when Joe's singing in the shower at the top of his lungs. Even this house isn't big enough to escape it." He moved back around the bed to crawl under the covers, offering Ellis warmth again. "Look, maybe staying here in the house where it's warmer will help buy you some extra days. And you're not alone this time. I'm not going anywhere, even if we're just friends and the spell sticks around. I'll help you hold on to you." Soft lips tasted wonderful in this gentle intimacy.

An abrupt sob and Ellis clung tight, wrapping both arms and legs around Galen, kisses and tears mingling on both their cheeks. Galen wondered at the intensity of it, until he stopped to think about *exactly* what Ellis had been through over the past year. The engineer in him had a million technical questions about how it happened in the first place, but right now Ellis needed comfort more than an interrogation, so Galen kept his consideration to the basics of Ellis's post-spell existence.

Out on a date, things go severely off the rails, and suddenly you're a frog. Aside from the shock and probably terror of *that*, you have zero instincts for the body you've been dumped into. You can't speak Frogish, so other frogs are useless—and onto the fact you're not actually one of them, so they're not friendly and possibly hostile. You don't know more than grade-school basics about what to eat, where or how to sleep. Three hundred miles from home, gone from a three-hour drive or five-hour train ride to hopping in three-foot increments. Maybe the length of one train stop before you start to dry out. Let alone the constant threat of being stepped on or eaten. Having no way to contact your family, and other humans ignoring you or freaking out. The thought of burying yourself alive in mud or water for the winter and trusting it will actually work. And waking to find you have to do it all over again. Fear, stress, fight-or-flight—for an entire year.

Good God. He pulled Ellis closer.

Nothing else registered until the grandfather clock in the hallway began its intricate chime of 2:00 a.m. Ellis pulled back, a hand to his chest, face pale in the warmth of the lamplight, breathing shallow. "Oh God, I can feel it coming on. I'm changing back." He pulled the sweatshirt off and dumped it on the floor. "Don't look. I don't know how it looks from outside… me."

"It's okay. I'm right here." Galen kissed him quickly, then closed his eyes and waited until the last chime faded into the night. He glanced down at Ellis's pillow. Sure enough, there sat the frog.

A deep sigh filled tiny lungs. "You may as well sleep. I need to soak at least an hour just to feel frog-normal again."

The technical questions would wait. Galen nodded, then reached over and stroked his fingers down over

Ellis's back, liking the shiver it caused. "It'll be okay, Ellis. I'll see you in the morning."

The quiet splash of water moving in the little terrarium lulled him to sleep.

SUNDAYS seemed to be a recovery day all around. From the safety of Galen's pocket, Ellis had watched Ben declare over breakfast that he'd be holed up in his office all day working on his doctoral dissertation. Joe had breezed through on his way to the glassed-in lap pool off one side of the back terrace. Later, from up in Galen's office with its wide bank of windows, he noted again the greenhouse-like fitness area forming one of the turrets at this end of the main floor.

What he *hadn't* seen yet was any evidence of the Townsend parents. Maybe they were the sort to travel most of the time now that their sons were grown? Maybe they'd moved to a condo in Palm Springs or some Greek island for the winter?

He mulled over asking while he caught up on *Thrones* and Galen puttered with the engine. They really knew very little about each other. Ellis couldn't shake the mental image of Mom or Dad waking up in the middle of the night and coming up to find out who the hell Galen was talking to. Or worse, who the hell was naked in bed with their youngest son.

That thought prodded him enough to pause the show before another episode started. It wasn't the first time today a break had become a few minutes' chat or banter, just talking as if he wasn't still a fucking frog. He waited until Galen looked up, one of those narrow brows quirking. "Um, is it just you and your brothers here right now? Haven't seen any sign of your folks. They on a cruise or something?"

The sudden tightening of Galen's shoulders and a bleakness in the blue eyes said more than any response could have, and Ellis wished he hadn't asked. "Oh. Oh God, I am so sorry, man."

One slim shoulder lifted, and Galen glanced away. "It's okay. You didn't know."

Ellis hopped over onto the worktable, needing to close the distance between them. "Do you mind if I ask what happened? I know it's real early between us for something so personal." But he'd rather do it now than reopen an obviously tender wound later.

Galen's gaze stayed on the work surface. "Car accident. They'd been on a holiday in New York City and were heading home before Hurricane Sandy hit. Just snow and ice and too many cars on the freeway. Someone cut off a semi and they got caught in the crossfire. Nothing terribly earth-shattering."

"It shattered yours." Ellis laid a foot on Galen's hand. "I'm sorry."

"Thanks." It took Galen a couple of minutes to compose himself again, rising to pace the length of his office, pausing to gaze at a few photographs displayed on the built-in bookshelves.

Ellis waited, his gut twisted in sympathy. He hadn't had that type of tragedy in his own life, but he had to wonder if this wasn't very much what his parents were going through over him. Though they were probably still holding out hope he was alive. Galen didn't have that.

A long gaze out over the back lawn and a few deep breaths seemed to have settled Galen enough for him to turn and sit back down at his worktable. "Sorry.

It still hits hard every once in a while. Even though we were old enough to be on our own, we were close, you know?"

"Not a thing wrong with deep emotion, dude. I'm rather partial to it myself where family's concerned." Time to ease them out of the abyss. "So, what's it like to grow up in a castle? You're way too familiar with the nooks and crannies of this place for it to have been a recent purchase. Or are you guys actually royalty in exile?"

Now a slow smile curved one corner of Galen's lips. "Nope. My folks built it this way."

"And they decided on a real castle, huh?" The smile encouraged, and Ellis hopped a little closer so he could look up into Galen's face. "Not that I'm complaining. It's what drew me to your house to begin with. But it does seem a little out of place in a Massachusetts suburb. What gives?"

Galen's breath puffed out in a soft chuckle. "*That* is one of the best stories of my parents' marriage. They went to Europe on their honeymoon and Mom fell in love with the castles in Germany. She wanted a place just like one, turrets and fancy halls, the odd suit of armor hanging around. Plenty of room for entertaining." The smile gained a few watts and the gaze went distant. "Probably a little showing off, though I don't remember Mom being like that very often. She was as likely to wade into a water fight with us or join in singing and dancing to 'YMCA' as she was to pull in a favor from The Capital Grille to cater a party and break out her one Oscar de la Renta and the Jimmy Choos." The smile had broadened by the time Galen finished and returned to the present. "Sorry. Wandered off on a tangent."

Ellis shrugged as best he could to demonstrate the apology wasn't necessary. "Sounds like you were close and she was pretty kickass." He patted Galen's hand again. "I'm guessing your dad wasn't as keen on the suits of armor, since I haven't seen one yet."

"George stands guard over Joe's files now." Galen laughed fully at Ellis's expression. "Anyway, you're right. Dad wanted a house, not a museum. A place they could actually live in and raise a family. They compromised. The main entry, the parlor, and the dining room could be the castle, turret for the staircase and all. *One* suit of armor. The rest of the house, including any guest bedrooms, would be built to live in. She could decorate the guest rooms however she wanted, but structurally they were just rooms." A stretch and more relaxation in Galen's form left Ellis feeling less like crawling under the sofa. "They ended up with a couple more turrets anyway, just more modern in actual use. After they died and we decided to do the consultancy out of the house, the setup was fairly ideal. Joe took the formal dining room for his office and moved downstairs to what used to be a guest suite by the kitchen. Ben has the entire owner's suite, which also includes an office. Joe's old bedroom suite up here doesn't get used much, but it's still furnished in case we have a client coming in who doesn't have extra budget for a hotel. We kept the foyer and parlor as is for the few times we entertain. We renovated a little— built a bypass to the mini-gym and sauna area, for example—but mostly it was cosmetic stuff. There's a lot of Mom and Dad still here."

"That's a terrific story." The evening light had shaded the house while they talked, and now Ellis felt the cold seeping into and under his skin. He crawled over to the little bungalow Galen had set up in his pool using the glass bowl and the desk lamp. The clock read six fifteen.

"Oh wow, it is getting dark. Lost track of time again." Galen began making last-second notes and putting his tools away. "You getting hungry? I can find some more sardines. I should just bring the rest of the case up to the kitchenette here. Save having to explain my sudden cravings, and it's not like Joe's going to miss them. He'll be happy to have them gone."

"Actually, I'd rather wait till nine and drag you out somewhere for a few hours." Ellis tried for a grin, not easy with frog sort-of-lips and zero teeth. "Probably shouldn't try for steak and dancing on a Sunday night with only a six-hour window, but I bet we could find a place for a light meal and a little mischief."

Those blue eyes popped wide. "You want to go out?"

Ellis shifted so the lamp would warm his other side without drying him out completely. "Why not? Like you said, we've got a little time. I may never be fully human again. Who knows, I may still transform even after I go into the pond to hibernate, in which case I'll likely drown before I ever wake up enough to get to the surface." The horrified expression *that* engendered made him rush on, since he couldn't currently wrap his arms around Galen. "I'd like to have one more really kickass night with someone I care about. Then we can hope for more."

Now the blue eyes brightened fully, and a new smile curled one side of Galen's mouth. "You sound a lot more optimistic than last night."

"What can I say? I forgot how dark *Thrones* is. Sorta makes my little predicament here, at least now that I've found you, seem a little less daunting."

Galen's smile grew more enchanting with each millimeter until Ellis forgot to breathe. "Well, we've still got a couple-plus hours. I could use a snack, and you don't want to pass out the moment you morph. I'll be right back."

"**GALEN?** Someone at the door for you."

Galen tucked his smirk away. Since it would have been hell trying to explain to his brothers that a date had been hiding in the house all day, Ellis had sneaked out the side door and around the garage to ring the front bell. No doubt Joe would catch some grief about leaving the gate at the street open again, but it was nothing new and well worth it.

He walked into the parlor to find Ellis shaking hands with Ben as Joe peered over his brother's shoulder. *Wow.*

Ellis's suit and shirt had been as complete a loss as the shoes, but he was about the same height as Joe, and just as lanky, so Galen had gone on a covert scrounge in the back of his brother's closet and come up with a pair of dark slacks and a pale green shirt that made Ellis's eyes glow brighter. His own socks and dress shoes finished the ensemble. Freshly showered and shaved, Ellis looked like he'd just walked off the cover of *GQ*. Galen had seen him less than ten minutes ago and was still stunned at the second look.

Galen covered his breathless reaction with pure brat. "Rollie. Hey."

Oh, the low-lidded glare was soooo worth it as well. Ellis squared his shoulders and favored Galen with an overdone nose-in-the-air. "Roland. As well you know and constantly ignore." Ellis had insisted on using his middle name as a pseudonym, probably because Ben had already seen his first and last names on the suit tag. "Are you ready to go?"

"Partying on a Sunday night?" Joe's brows popped up. "Who are you and where's the pod?"

Galen rolled his eyes. "It's just dinner. Lay off." He caught the light in Ben's eyes, approval and a bit of relief clear. "See, I'm not a complete hermit yet."

Little nod, little smile. "Enjoy yourselves." Ben turned and poked Joe in the ribs. "Come on, brother. You owe me a billiards game. And hopefully the ten bucks I lost last week."

Joe snorted and headed toward the game room, taking the front stairs two at a time. "In your dreams, moneyman. I am on a winning streak."

Galen took in Ellis's grin with a shrug and clasped lean fingers with his own. "Welcome to my world. Let's go. I know a good place for what you have in mind."

"YOU sure you don't want something a little more substantial?" Galen glanced at his own grilled chicken and then at Ellis's pasta primavera. "You never said you were a vegetarian."

"Dude, I've eaten enough algae and unconventional wildlife to last a lifetime. The taste buds could use a switch-up." Ellis stretched out on his side of the booth at the back of the slowly emptying restaurant, all long legs and arms. "Though I have to admit, the earthworms gave me a whole new set of thoughts to play with." A little moan teased the back of Ellis's throat as he closed his eyes. "That long, juicy body going down my throat a little at a time...."

Galen's whole nervous system twitched, jerking the fork in his hand.

An epic smirk curved those soft lips. "You are so easy to mess with." Pale green eyes twinkled at him. "Loving that."

The urge to call his friend a brat died in that gaze. His nervous system sent a few more twitches out, mostly a shiver up the insides of his thighs. He had to swallow for more than the food in his mouth before he could answer. "And revenge is every bit as satisfying. You just wait'll we get—"

"Oh. My. God." A voice from nearby cut into their banter. "Ellis Faraday? Is that really you? Good God man, your folks are going apeshit looking for you. What the fuck already?" A solid, athletic-looking lady in a dark pantsuit approached them, fortunately from close enough her questions hadn't crossed the entire restaurant, staring at Ellis.

Galen had watched Ellis's face pale a couple of shades, but now a deep breath brought back some color and a cool gaze surveyed the newcomer with one raised eyebrow. "I am ever so sorry, miss, but you have me confused with someone else." A broad, relaxed Southern accent jarred the voice Galen was used to in a… not unpleasant way. "My name is Roland Merriweather. Of the Savannah Merriweathers. Perhaps you've heard of us."

She blinked. "Seriously?" Several more moments passed as they stared at each other, Ellis's eyebrow remaining in its hover. Then she caved. "Oh. Sorry. You just… it's uncanny how much you look like Ellis. He's been missing for over a year, and it's hard on his folks. Pretty sure they've torn through half the family fortune looking for him." She glanced down, clearly embarrassed. "I'm sorry to have disturbed your meal." Her shoulders slumped as she walked away.

Galen waited until she was out of earshot before considering his friend, who was toying with his pasta far less enthusiastically than before. "Why? And a Southern accent?"

"Year of summer stock, just for something to do." Pasta and vegetables made a few more rounds of the plate before Ellis spoke again. "You heard her. That was Dena Goodayle. We went to high school together, though I was a couple years ahead. My hair was darker then. I'm surprised she—" Ellis paused for a sip of wine, and Galen could see a shine in his eyes even though Ellis didn't look up. "She used to come over and exercise Mom's horses. I'd guess she must still, or she stays in touch. She said… well, you heard. I don't want anyone to know where I am until I'm sure the spell's broken. I mean, can you imagine if I frog-morphed right in front of my parents? Seriously?"

"Ah." He supposed it made sense. Given the history of Ellis's journey…. Galen watched pure grief and a fair dose of guilt play across his friend's face. Yeah, he'd feel the same way, knowing his folks were worrying about him and not daring to make contact yet.

Ellis poked at his dinner some more. "This was a bad idea, coming out. I just never expected anyone I know to be down here."

"No reason you should have." Galen laid down his fork and reached for Ellis's hand. "Let's get it boxed up. We can go eat down at the gazebo with a couple beers. The guys will have traded pool for a movie by now, or they've called it a night if they've got early work stuff tomorrow. So nobody but you and me with the last of the fireflies and a blanket. It's barely ten now." He'd do anything to brighten the dark mood he could see settling over Ellis.

A smile slid from one corner of Ellis's full mouth to the other. "I do like the sound of that. You might be as smart as those work glasses of yours make you look."

Galen signaled for the check and pulled out his wallet. "Done and done."

"JOE'S clothes fit you pretty good in a pinch." With one blanket beneath them on the bench seat and another over their legs, Galen's arm around his shoulders felt amazing. The matching ottoman made it a cozy lounge. "I'll grab you some things when I go out for that engine part tomorrow."

"You don't have to—" Ellis huffed at the half glare he got. "Okay, okay, I'll quit arguing."

"Good." Galen set the takeout boxes farther out of the way on one of the little side tables, then pulled Ellis closer and slid long fingers up into his hair. "I have a better use for both our mouths." The hand not causing divine sensations at the base of his skull pulled the oversized blanket up over their chests. "And hands."

Ellis gasped as a slightly chilled touch wandered under his borrowed dress shirt, only to have his mouth plundered with the sort of precision he'd expect from an engineer. Fuck, it was good!

He'd fought this with Galen beyond the very basics, allowing himself to touch and be touched again. And it did feel amazing. Actually, it felt downright fucking perfect, despite the fact they still knew jack shit about each other. But what if he never fully changed back? What the hell kind of life would that be, human for six hours in the latest part of the night and the rest as a frog? He'd never be able to hold a job, finish school.... What sort of a life was that for a partner to share?

What if this is what you need to break *the spell?*

Galen's hand under his shirt had warmed considerably as they kissed and was currently derailing his train of worries. Now it explored, undoing the buttons, stroking, teasing, worrying one of his nipples until Ellis thought he'd pass out. Pure want coiled his gut and left his dick pulsing for the first time in a year.

"Mmm." Galen freed Ellis's mouth and trailed a long kiss along his jaw up to his ear. "God, you taste fantastic. Am I going too fast for you? I know I said we should take it easy, but...."

Ellis wrapped his own fingers around Galen's bicep, the corded muscle feeling every bit as good on his palm as the warm fleece did on the back of his hand. He found the bottom edge of Galen's sweater. "This is fairly easy. And wonderful." He returned kisses along the edge of Galen's late-day shadow of beard, sighing at the luxury he'd almost forgotten. "And warm. God, I feel genuinely warm for the first time in months."

"You're not going to be cold like that ever again." Galen spread his hand flat over Ellis's stomach, fingertips just skimming the waistband of the borrowed trousers. "Even if you have to hibernate, we'll rig something up so you can be right in my room." Soft lips nibbled the hollow of Ellis's collarbone, the shirt collar pushed aside as much as Galen could. Words vibrated over his skin. "Terrarium or something. I'm not leaving you on your own."

His fingers tingled over velvety sweater fibers and then smooth skin, tracing the bumps up Galen's spine.

He lost track of... pretty much anything... as they kissed and caressed.

But soon the now-familiar sensation of his body contracting prompted undressing in a way he didn't find fun at all. Galen still showered him with soft words, gentle support. He pressed one last kiss to Galen's lips. "Close your eyes. I don't want you to watch."

It was a bit like going down a dark water-slide tunnel, only the end kept getting smaller and smaller until he found clear sight again from one corner of the ottoman. The chill breeze didn't leave him shivering anymore, only drowsy.

Galen had gotten up and was gathering the clothes Ellis had discarded. "It's all good. I set my own hours most of the time. The guys will be off to their stuff. We'll just sleep in till —" A glance at a decent watch brought a gasp. "Ellis, it's 3:00 a.m."

"What?" Surely the oncoming hibernation instinct was messing with his hearing. "I thought I heard you say—"

"Three. It's *three*." Galen scooped him up and tucked him into a fold of the borrowed shirt, giving him a kiss on the nose. "You gained a whole hour!" He set the pile of clothes back on the bench and turned to fold up the big fleece blankets. "It's working! It's really working!"

Ellis allowed hope to flare for one glorious moment. Then he hauled it back and stomped it into its box for safekeeping. "Maybe. I still feel winter pulling at me, though. If I was fully human again, I'd expect that pull to be for a ski slope rather than a duck pond." He shifted against the shirt, feeling the moisture seeping out of his skin. He'd have to soak once they got back to the house. "At least the morph included taking care of the hard-on you gave me. Frogs don't have dicks, exactly. There's something at least. No tiny blue balls." He hadn't planned on that coming out quite as bitter as it sounded, but....

Galen's brows drew together as if he'd argue for a little more optimism. Then he nodded, ignoring the bad joke. "I get it. I do." He tucked the folded blankets back into their basket and scooped up Ellis-with-clothes in one hand and the takeout boxes in the other. "Well, I'll just have to be hopeful enough for us both right now. Let's go get you into a quick soak and then we'll sleep. Tomorrow will look better."

Dear God, I love him. Already. After two days. Or at least something not limited solely to gratitude and basic lustful attraction. But clearly one-way love or lust or whatever wasn't going to cut it. Ellis could feel every second dragging him closer to a date with a watery— He could only pray it wouldn't *really* be a grave this time.

Chapter Six

ON Monday, they slept in until nearly ten. Galen ran his errands and finished his work on the Gyro Systems engine and client report while Ellis alternately sunned and soaked in his dish and *Thrones* played itself on the TV screen. A new minimal wardrobe now lay on Galen's bed, waiting patiently for 9:00 p.m.

As predicted, Galen's brothers were out for long stretches of time, popping in occasionally to fill Galen in on various clients. A makeshift screen, improvised from the FedEx box and a stack of books, kept Joe from seeing the frog in the room. All in all, a fairly chill day.

He couldn't help it. It didn't matter if he was watching from across the room or the corner of the desk, if they were talking or he just watched Galen

putter with—and mutter at, which just added a new
level of cute—the engine. Every moment Ellis could
feel his heart slipping a little further into far more than
gratitude and attraction. A real friendship, a genuine
affection… and leaning to more.

You're an idiot. It was just as likely that Warlock
Wayne had been screwing with him, was *still* screwing
with him, and there wasn't actually a cure. Just this
limbo for the rest of his life. Wayne hadn't given him
any instructions, and little in the way of *if* there was
even a cure outside of the bastard's own warped mind.
Ellis was running on an assumption built out of fairy
tales four centuries old. And he and Galen barely knew
each other anyway, no matter he was seeing the other
man at his "worst," all the little everyday habits a date
could hide for months. What the hell made Ellis think
this was anything more than basic human decency and
a little mutual lust? All the insecurities from last night
resumed their race around the walls of his brain.

"You're thinking. Hard. Funny how I can tell that
when not much of your face moves as a frog." Galen
smiled from his perch at the worktable, elbow on
the surface and hand propping his head. "You're not
the only one thinking hard. I try to focus on this and
instead find myself staring at you and remembering
last night. Not getting work done at my usual pace,
but I'm liking it." He reached over and stroked the
length of Ellis's back.

God! The insecurities vaporized in a wash of
sensation.

"You doing okay?"

He tried for cool and casual, but a croaking groan
got away from him and so did the unvarnished truth.
"You keep doing that and I'll be plenty okay."

The low chuckle and mischievous smile didn't help. "Well, it's nearly eight. I put in a delivery order for nine. Nice seafood place. Told the guys I was feeling hermit-y and I'd fend for myself tonight. Happens a few times a month, so they won't be suspicious yet. Hopefully by the time we'd have to figure out another excuse, we won't have to." Galen didn't bother using both hands to put away his tools, keeping one on Ellis while he cleared the worktable. "We'll pull out the candles and make a proper date of it." The last pencil settled in the cup, and those nimble fingers began to massage in tiny circles back up his spine. "So I suppose I could get you warmed up as well."

Ellis supposed there really ought to be something slightly weird about—okay, platonic areas, but wow—foreplay when he was still in amphibian form, but for the life of him he couldn't get his brain to form any sort of protest. Shit, that was a good spot! Ellis felt his whole froggy form sort of dissolve into jelly. If he could have turned over like a puppy, he would have. He let his nerve endings take over and blank his brain.

By the time Galen brought the pseudo-pond into the bedroom and went to set their little private table, Ellis barely managed the coherence to make the short span of hops from his dish to the bed before the clock in the hall struck nine and he found himself dragged back up the metaphorical tunnel to human form. *Wow*. He felt incredible after that massage, and quite inclined to tell Galen to forget dinner and simply take him to bed. A quick shower left him warm and feeling even more relaxed. And his legs didn't hurt. For the second morph in a row. So the stretches when he was in frog form were helping the transition. Or it was the shorter time between morphs. Either way, he felt goddamned fantastic.

He'd just finished dressing and finger-combing his hair when Galen came in from the private balcony attached to the bedroom. "Dinner's here. It's all set up and read— Shit."

"What?" Ellis looked down, panic crashing over him. "What? Did something not change this time? Am I still sprouting frog ears? What?"

"You really weren't kidding when you said prince." Galen came over and brushed a strand of hair out of Ellis's eyes. "Man, you scrub up nice. I saw you scrubbed up just last night, and you're even more gorgeous now. And frogs don't have external ears. You taught me that." A hungry kiss left Ellis breathless.

"Oh." He figured that was his limit on the eloquent scale at the moment; relief left him far more interested in the sensations he'd been privy to earlier.

Better to wrap his arm around Galen's waist and pull the man close enough to feel everything. Better still to push the button-down collar aside and settle his tongue against the hollow of Galen's throat. *You know what? Screw the fucking spell.* Tonight, even if it was just for a few hours, he was going to enjoy being a man again. And the heat between them was clearly mutual. Consenting adults and all.

"God, Ellis…."

Oh yeah, plenty going on where their hips met. Ellis got a handful of firm, round ass and squeezed, grinning as Galen gasped. Sky-blue eyes rolled back and drifted shut at the same time. Ellis let his touch drift down to the inside of a lean thigh and was rewarded with a genuine whimper. If he could have reached farther from where they were standing, dinner would have gone cold by the time they came up for air, but....

He eased back slowly, liking the way Galen had all but melted into him. The curve of Galen's ear teased his lips as he spoke. "Since you went to the trouble of ordering dinner, I suppose we should eat it. Then maybe we can find other things for dessert. If you're amenable."

He counted seven shaky breaths before Galen's eyes cleared, three more before Galen's knees appeared to support weight again. "Yeah. I... uh... yeah. Shit. Wow. Yeah. Eat." Galen swallowed hard a couple times. "Shit. Yeah."

The laugh bubbled up from somewhere deep in his gut, the first Ellis could remember since the world went to hell. "Love it when I can reduce a quip-meister to single-word sentences. Guess I haven't lost my touch."

"No. No, you haven't. God." Galen still seemed to be having issues seeing clearly, though that bulge in his dress jeans had no problem making itself known. Long fingers gripped the doorframe to the balcony. A new muttered whisper likely wasn't meant for Ellis to hear. "Shit."

Ellis felt a smile stretch his lips. Definitely time to eat.

HOLY *shit.* Overjoyed Ellis wasn't in one of his depressed waves, but wow.... Galen's knees still shook from the gut-searing, brain-melting clinch they'd just shared. Other parts of his anatomy practically vibrated against his clothing, making any sort of coherence damn near impossible. Conversation was going to be a royal bitch.

Hell, getting over to a chair at the little candlelit table he'd set up took a concerted effort. And the self-satisfied smirk riding Ellis's lips did not help. Mojo had clearly not been a problem for his frog prince.

Galen had never really considered himself either dom or sub; he'd topped as often as he'd bottomed and wasn't averse to an occasional mild kink or two, depending on the personality of his partner. But lord, the urge to drop to his knees and beg Ellis… actually warred quite nicely with the desire to tie the brat to his four-poster and tease until Ellis screamed. At the moment begging appealed more, simply because he couldn't get his brain on track enough to formulate a proper torture.

"Hey, you weren't kidding. This is fantastic. And I should be sick of seafood by now." Oblivious—or acting so—to Galen's continued lack of oxygen and functioning brain cells, Ellis dug into his dinner with fair gusto. "God, you have no idea how amazing this feels. Clean clothes—hell, *actual* clothes, holding a fucking fork, seeing the world from more than six inches off the ground." A curious foot in its new loafer rubbed against Galen's ankle. "Gorgeous company."

"Yeah." God, had his voice really cracked like when he was fourteen? Galen opted for a sip of his wine before he fought for words again.

"And salad! Oh my God, crisp vegetables! I am in heaven. Sheer fucking heaven." Ellis's foot continued its massage as he gushed, the smirk bright in his eyes even when he wasn't making eye contact.

Okay, that's how the evening was set to go. *Brat.* Good thing Galen loved a challenge, because plotting

X-rated revenge amid the sensual onslaught took a level of forced focus he hadn't needed in a long time. He'd forgotten how much fun it was... and how incredibly hard. In more ways than one.

Frustrating Ellis by pretending the ankle massage—and the innuendo mixed in with the re-celebrating of All Things Human—had little effect on him left Galen hiding his own smirk. He could live a lifetime with this sort of friendly warfare.

Don't get ahead of yourself. He's got family waiting for him and some sort of heirdom to claim. You barely know each other and there's no guarantees here, no matter what you promised. That eased him out of the sexual haze a bit. Either the spell never fully broke and Ellis would be trapped as a frog for large portions of each day, or the spell did break and Ellis would go back to his old life. Both choices left them separated from any type of full relationship.

Just enjoy tonight. It's been months since you were with someone. Galen took the last bite of his fish and realized Ellis was staring at him, elegant hands folded together in front of an empty plate and a quieter smile than the imp of before. Galen lifted one shoulder in apology. "Sorry. Brain took a side street. How long have I been zoned?"

"Couple minutes." Ellis's foot hadn't stopped its exploration of Galen's ankle. "Where'd you go, anyway? The expressions crossing your face were... interesting. Sort of sad toward the end. What?"

Another shrug to push away what he couldn't control. "Dunno. Nothing specific. I can do that sometimes, just be looking out over the lawns and lose all conscious awareness." He reached across the small table and took Ellis's hand. "Are you finished torturing my feet and ready to move on to something else?"

Long fingers twined with his. "I can think of a tangent or two." Ellis rose, pulling Galen up with him, moving close as a soft ballad started playing from the AI assistant on the desk inside. Lean hips pressed closer, shifting against him in time with the music. "Something else I've missed." He rested Galen's hand against his chest, wrapped it with his own hand. "Mind if I lead?"

So hard to remember this was all just temporary when they fit together so well and Ellis's faint stubble teased his cheek, then his lips. When warm hands found their way under his clothing, when his own found smooth skin. When a few danced circles brought them back to his bedside. He sighed against Ellis's mouth, tongues tangled, while he slid his fingertips up Ellis's spine.

A shiver and a groan made him smile. "God, you melted me doing that when I was a fucking frog. You have got a hell of a touch, Galen Townsend." Ellis hadn't stopped kissing as he spoke, and the words vibrated clear to Galen's back teeth.

He left Ellis's mouth and began to work on the buttons of Ellis's shirt with his tongue. Time... they didn't have a lot, but he had enough to take things slow and sensual. To feast rather than devour. He didn't want a quick romp. He wanted... well, as much of everything as was possible. Tonight, and other brief nights like this, might be all they had. Or tonight *would* be all they had.

And falling for a guy he barely knew, frog or not, was just crazy. So he'd enjoy the time they had and keep a firm hold on his heart.

A few crisp hairs tickled his lips and nose as he finished the last button at Ellis's belt buckle. Working his way back up, he lingered in the channels between a softly defined six-pack, took his time sucking each dark nipple until they pebbled hard against his tongue. The hollow of Ellis's throat and the curve of his jaw let him meander back to that delicious mouth, noting the other man's pulse hammering through his carotid.

His own sweater vanished over his head, but Galen didn't pause longer than absolutely necessary. The belt buckle opened easily for him; the dress slacks slid down over Ellis's hips and pooled on the floor. Galen cupped firm ass muscles and pulled Ellis tight against his erection. "I want you. I want us. For as long as we can."

LOSING the rest of their clothing took moments. Ellis pushed Galen back onto the turned-down bed, pausing to admire his lover. "You… I…."

"Yeah. Skip talking now."

Gladly. Galen had him at "want you." Ellis knelt on the bed, straddling those long legs. Much as he would like to make things last for hours, it was already midnight. And the last thing he wanted was to get to the verge of orgasm only to morph back to frog at the last second. A, he didn't want to do that to Galen, and B, despite the okay-morph after cuddling from last night, he wasn't entirely sure what a human-size case of full-blown *coitus interruptus* would do to a frog body and didn't fancy finding out the hard way.

Still, there was time to make his lover feel good. And he'd never had a problem making partners of either gender feel really good. Ellis settled his mouth into the

hollow of Galen's throat, trailing kisses down, using his
tongue and teeth to full advantage. At the same time,
he stroked up long thighs and lean hips, loving every
gasp, moan, and curse elicited. Digging his thumbs into
the hard muscles of Galen's quads rewarded him with
a plea.

"God, please...."

He hummed reassurance over satiny skin, sucking
at one pink nipple as his massage wandered higher
into silky curls just above Galen's erection. A little
extra pressure there prompted a whimper and the push
of those hips against his touch. *Oh yeah, that's so
perfect.*

The fact that Galen wasn't returning his touch
left him grinning. The man probably couldn't form a
coherent brain signal to his fingers right now. Breathing
sounded like it might be taking a lot of concentration
as well. It became a sob when Ellis settled thumb and
forefinger at the base of a rock-hard dick and began to
massage again.

"Ellis...." Barely a whisper, but it shot straight to
his heart.

"Yeah. Yeah, I know. We're gonna be really good."
He blew a soft breath over Galen's tip and got another
whimper for his effort. "Nightstand?"

"Mmhmm...."

Slipping on a condom took little time and gave
him a chance to just stare at Galen for a minute. Eyes
closed, arousal so very evident, breath speeding,
fingers curled in the blankets... beautiful. Perfect.
Ellis knew his heart teetered a knife's edge from
falling seriously in love. Not just because of the sex or
the friendship or the belief in his completely jacked-
up story, but all of it. Ellis could *picture* years with

Galen. And that was trouble if said jacked-up story didn't have a happy ending.

"Ellis, please." A shiver worked its way up over Galen's body. "Please. Cold without you...."

Ellis shook out of his thoughts and covered that lean body with his own again. "Sorry, babe, got lost staring at you for a minute." He gathered Galen's arousal against his own and began to stroke. "Let's get warm again."

"Ohgodyeah...." Galen burrowed against Ellis's throat, tongue massaging circles in rhythm with his thrust into Ellis's hand.

The clock struck one as Ellis eased up, reaching back into the nightstand for lube so he could explore tight heat, his own body pleading for release. Joining left him breathless, sightless except for a rain of white sparkles. A slow pull back and a deep thrust finished off even that visibility. Long legs gripped his shoulders, a muffled groan evidence Galen had buried his face in a pillow. That alone reminded him to cover his own mouth as release ripped through him, the warm wet of his lover's orgasm spreading over his stomach.

He barely had the energy to find the wastebasket and a shirt from the floor to clean up enough they wouldn't stick together. Galen's embrace welcomed him, the covers he pulled up warm around them. Drowsy words vibrated Ellis's skin. "S'perfect...."

And the final bastion of common sense toppled. *I love you, Galen Townsend.* If only he dared say it aloud or hope it might be returned. He drifted off with it looping in his mind.

Chapter Seven

GALEN stretched, bright fall sunshine streaming in through the windows. But definitely too cold for comfort. He got up to close the patio doors they'd left open overnight, then turned back to the bed. Empty. No long lean form curled up, though there was plenty of evidence that he hadn't slept alone. And no frog in the makeshift pond. What the—

"Galen! Since when do you sleep in past nine on a weekday?" Ben's voice echoed up from downstairs. "Get your ass in gear. I have a phone conference with Gyro and I need your notes."

"Yeah, sorry. I've got them right here." He shuffled into his sleep pants, half felt his way from bedroom to office, nearly broke his nose trying to walk through the client/work area dividers rather than the space between them, and grabbed the file from his desk before Ben could get up the stairs. They met in the wide hallway with its chess table and conversation area. "Sorry, man, restless night. Slept lousy." Not true, but similar enough in symptoms to *mind-blowing sex until the wee hours of the morning*. And he still wasn't really coherent, because where the hell was Ellis? Shower, maybe?

"That sucks. But you better get that engine and blueprint packed up and call FedEx. We're on a tight timetable with these guys." Ben glanced over the file. "Nice. Mr. Wizard works his magic once more. Joe's already off to a meeting with Torres for the Q-Smart thing, and I have six phone or video calls between now and noon. Then it's back to the dissertation."

"I still need to finish the blueprint, just the labeling, but I'll get it in the mail tomorrow. The engine can go today. After that, my board's clear for the next few days." Galen forced his brain back to work for a moment. "Puts me on dinner duty tonight. Ordering Chinese okay?"

"Works." Ben was already halfway back down the stairs, mind elsewhere.

Galen returned to his room. No water running in the ensuite bath. He gathered up clothes and tossed them in the hamper, then decided they hadn't mucked up the bed enough to bother changing the sheets quite yet. Molly wouldn't be back until Wednesday. Pulling the sheet and blanket straight together, he moved a pillow out of the way.

A frog, looking far less shiny than any amphibian ought to, sat on the mattress, lidless eyes focused… not really anywhere. Galen rested his hand on the small back and flinched. Dry… terribly, terribly dry.

"Ellis? Are you okay?" No response, though Galen could still see the frog's throat moving slowly. What the hell? The baking dish pond sat in its normal spot, well within hopping distance. "Ellis!" He scooped up the frog and set him in the water, heart hammering. *Oh, God, did we... did I...?* "Ellis, come on, talk to me, croak at me, *something*!"

"Ribbit. Happy now?" No brat-banter. Nothing, really. Ellis hadn't moved. He just sat there, barely floating.

"Oh God, thank you." Galen dropped the pillow in the middle of the half-made bed and sat down. "Are you okay?"

The golden eyes fixed him with a weary sideways glare. "I'm a fucking frog again, asshole. After all that last night. What do you think?"

A retort started across his lips, but Galen swallowed it and took a breath. *I probably would feel the same if it were me.*

Ellis sighed. "Sorry."

"No, it's okay. I get it. But I don't get why you didn't go back to your water when—" A wave of horror knotted his gut as Galen stared at the space on the bed where Ellis had been sitting... *drying out.*

"No. Don't you dare." The very thought of it closed up Galen's voice to a tight whisper that had very little oxygen behind it. His insides iced over, and he grabbed hold of the corner of the mattress before he gave in to the impulse to grab Ellis instead and probably hug him to a literal pulp. His voice hadn't improved and had gained a great deal of excess moisture. He didn't bother wiping away the itch of tears down his cheek. "Don't you dare. Ellis, *no*."

Another sigh. "Galen, last night was a hell of a lot more than a jump in the sack. I felt it. I'll admit to wishful thinking in believing you did as well. And yet here I am. Don't even know if we made it to three o'clock in the morning again. I woke up at six like this." The slightest push of a webbed foot turned the little back fully to Galen. "Wayne was screwing with me. There's no break for the spell. I can't do this anymore."

Galen managed to swallow enough to get oxygen to his voice, not caring right now if his face was still wet. "Of course I felt it as well. I don't—I wouldn't—I mean... yes, I felt it too. And you were human at five when I managed just enough brain battery to go use the toilet. I remember because you cuddled up to me when I got back and muttered something about dragonflies." He swallowed again and felt his lips curve into half a grin. "Had some nice dreams after that, thanks."

"See, that's what I mean. I can't do this anymore, and I sure as hell can't do it to you. What the hell kind of relationship would it be, if we even want to go there, that would— Wait. Five?" Ellis turned back with a splash, hope lighting those golden eyes at last. "You mean—"

"We're making something happen. Maybe not everything, but something. And I meant what I said. You're not alone. You're not going to be alone ever again, whether we end up as just friends or more." Galen dipped his fingers in the water and smoothed some over Ellis's back. "Now, I'm going to grab a shower and then get you some sardines. When I get back, I expect you to look less like a museum specimen." He raised a brow for effect. "Got it?"

A more-wet-than-before snort rewarded him. "If you're waiting for a 'Yes, sir,' you're not getting it."

"That's more like it." He set the little pond over where it would get some sun, his gut unknotting and his heart settling back to normal. "Now, let's get the day under way."

THE rest of Monday and all day Tuesday passed without much fanfare. The Gyro engine and later the blueprint were packed and sent on their way. Ben and Joe had solid days of field meetings, so they had the big house to themselves. Galen had nothing else on his work board, so he fixed the brakes on Joe's Audi and changed the oil on his Corvette and Ben's Porsche.

Ellis still didn't want Galen to watch him morph, and with the crushing disappointment after their first time fully making love, they'd decided it was better on Ellis's psyche to hold off on more than moderate-to-heavy petting. But it didn't matter. They talked when he was a frog, cuddled when he was a human, and the rest of the world went on its way mostly unheeded. And with each day, they gained an hour.

At 7:30 on Wednesday morning, Ellis listened to breakfast conversation from the base of the railing where the pub-themed game room looked down over the vaulted, open-space family room, kitchen, and dining room. He couldn't see Galen and his brothers— the overlook began at the family room—but he could clearly hear their voices and smell the pancakes and coffee.

The family room was a casual showpiece, but Ellis had no problem imagining three small boys tumbling through the space, pizza parties and game nights, afternoon homework with snacks, controlled chaos. A two-story fireplace dominated the far wall, its raised hearth continuing in benches holding up the bookcases that flanked either side. Big, solid furniture designed to be lived on filled the space with warm reds, browns, and golds, the occasional pop of blue or green. Chess and card tables sat ready for battle, and on the left wall a built-in closet with glass doors held a mountain of board games and puzzles. On the right, tall windows and french doors looked out onto the back terrace, half-sheltered by the upstairs veranda.

He grinned as best he could when his attention returned to the conversation and realized the chaos hadn't ever really stopped.

"It's going to take me getting in his face. I can tell." The soft shriek of a fork against ceramic preceded a pause and the slight thickening of Joe's voice after swallowing. "I've already got the flight and a hotel booked for tonight. If I'm lucky I'll be home Friday."

"Jesus Christ, I thought we were all but finished with InuTile." The scrape of a chair and the Doppler effect on Ben's voice indicated motion. "What the hell is McPeek doing now?" The sound of liquid pouring and a *clink-thud* informed Ellis that the eldest Townsend brother had refilled his coffee.

Joe's eyeroll translated perfectly. "You know how it took us forever to come up with a product name because he absolutely insisted some form of 'inulin' had to be used? Like the average consumer has a clue what that means. It's a fucking prebiotic that slows down your digestion so you can absorb more nutrients, but it doesn't constipate you. That's all anyone needs to know. But no, he *has* to have it in his product name. Then he thinks 'tile' sounds cool, let's use InuTile."

"I've always thought that makes it sound like insulation board." Galen's comment held laughter behind the casual delivery.

"Yeah, well, he insisted it was either that or InuLase, which I had to kibosh because it's too close to something already out there that's an entirely different substance, and I had to tell him *that* six times before it sank in." Another chair scrape, and Ellis adjusted his position on the balcony base so he wasn't spotted as Joe paced the family room area. "Now he tells me he wants to market in eastern Canada as well as here in the US. You know what *inutile* means in French when you see it instead of hearing that long *i* sound?"

"I took Spanish and Ben did German, bro. But I'm guessing nothing good."

"Useless! It literally means 'useless.' You can't sell the Chevy Nova in Spain or Mexico, you don't try to sell Vicks chest rub in Germany, the UK frowns on using 'Wang Cares' as a tagline, and you sure as hell aren't going to be able to sell InuTile in eastern Canada!" Joe flung himself onto one of the overstuffed sofas and groaned at the vaulted ceiling. "*Why* did the universe see fit to saddle me with a fucking idiot?"

Clearly the middle Townsend brother had no problem with high drama now and again. Ellis kept his laughter to himself.

"Must be all that clean living, Joe." Galen took the *fuck-off* glare with a smile, as it was already on his face when he walked into view to ruffle his brother's hair. "You'll pull it off. You always do. Just remind him that if we consult beyond the budgeted contract hours, it counts as overtime. That might shake him up."

"Yeah, I know. It's just a pain in the ass. And I've seen the research. The stuff actually does what he says it does. If I can just get him to *listen*...." Joe levered himself up off the sofa and moved toward a door between the game closet and the back stairs where the overlook began. "Anyway, I gotta pack and reschedule three other accounts so I can go work the magic on him. Tell Molly I'll bring her roses as an apology if she does my wash today. I'll set the hamper in the laundry room before the Uber gets here. By the way, what happened to that case of sardines? I was going to dump them, but they're not in the pantry where I left them. Somebody get a craving?"

"Local shelter called yesterday, hoping for a donation to their drive. Told them we'd send a check, and they said their cats would be happy to polish off the sardines for us." Galen's easy half truth worked. The sardines *would* get eaten, and Ellis had no doubt that the shelter would get its check and any fish left over if the spell broke.

"Just make sure you get in McPeek's face tactfully. If he balks he's likely to take Pomales and Murray with him, and we just got them settled into the process." The clink of dishes indicated Ben clearing the table and filling the dishwasher.

"Yeah, yeah, I know. Finish the primal scream here. When I get back, I expect Beef Wellington at Abe & Louie's for putting up with this bullshit." The snark lost its bite in the gleam of Joe's smile. "Later, guys." He closed the door behind him.

"He has a real fetish going with their steaks. What's on your plate for today, Ben?" Galen, still in the family room, glanced up at the railing and smiled as he saw Ellis. A quick glance toward Ben, then Galen gave him a wink before moving back into the kitchen. "Work or school?"

"It's mid-October. The annual pre-holidays Tornado Run cleaning spree. Molly will be here at nine on the dot, and she'll tear through here with her vacuum, mop, and furniture polish like Seal Team Six. I won't be able to hear myself think." The affection in Ben's gripe made Ellis smile again. "I purposely scheduled a business meeting with Murray today, and I'm going to haul my dissertation stuff along so I can hide at the library until at least four. You vacating as well?"

"Somebody's got to man the landline. I'm good." Galen reappeared to scoop up a book and put it back on one of the shelves by the fireplace. "If it gets too hazardous, I can escape outside for a while. It's still warm enough. With Gyro done I feel like taking a day."

"Sounds like a plan. Let's eat out of the freezer tonight. I'm feeling a yen to power-cook again, and I'll need all the space I can get." Ben walked into view to grab another book off the coffee table, then disappeared under the overlook again. "By the way, thanks for the oil change."

"You can pay me with a double batch of those empanadas you made last month," Galen called after him. "I'll put chorizo and green olives on the shopping list." The kitchen light went off, and Galen paused at the foot of the back stairs before shouting again. "I'll text you the pantry staples before noon so you can add what you need." A faint and unintelligible agreement echoed back.

That level of order in a house full of bachelors left Ellis shaking his head... ish. "You guys are so organized it's scary."

"We've been well-trained." Galen grinned up at the balcony again. "I can still hear Joe griping clear through his bedroom door."

Ellis snorted. "He always like that? Diva ready to blow?"

"Nah, he moves at Warp Ten but he's usually pretty chill. He just has a low tolerance for high-maintenance clients. We let him blow here so he doesn't blow at them." Galen bounded up the stairs and reappeared at the game room's kitchenette in the same time it took Ellis to cross the span from the balcony. "At least we won't have to worry about dodging him for a couple days. Ben won't freak out at the sight of a frog. He might put you outside in the garden, but I'll find you."

"How about the housekeeper?" Ellis aimed for a barstool and chuckled when Galen stuck out a hand and caught him instead. "Nice move."

"Anytime." Galen stroked once down Ellis's back, igniting nerves again, then set Ellis on his shoulder. "Molly? Not sure. I don't think we ever had wild critters in the house when we were kids. Plenty of room out on the veranda, and Mom always told us we had to return them home when we were done looking at them."

"I think I'd have liked your folks." A bubble of mischief rose up, and Ellis had to absorb the recoil as he flicked his tongue onto Galen's earlobe with the same accuracy he'd developed for dragonflies.

"Ew! Come on!"

"Closest I can get to a kiss right now." He crawled closer to Galen's ear. "That bad, really?"

"Can't you do it slower? Felt like a small sledgehammer." Galen rubbed at his earlobe. "I think you might have pierced it. Do I need to get an earring now?"

"It's not a spear, it's a tongue. Not even a forked one." Ellis nosed against Galen's fingers. "Sorry. To do it slower I'd have to be like *in* your ear. I've got close-range or Javelin missile. Nothing between. Didn't realize just how much of a punch it packed. Figured the bugs were a little more fragile than a human. My bad."

"It's okay. But we better hold that thought until tonight." Galen headed around the corner toward his bedroom and office. "Let's get some basic cleanup done before Molly lands. We'll be manning the phone, but mostly we can just hang out."

"Works for me."

IS that…? It is." Ellis peered down the wide hallway from Galen's bedroom toward the game room. Five doors lined the wall opposite—four regular wood, and one metal with a button panel to one side. How the hell had he missed that over the last few days? Then again, things had been kind of crazy. "That's an *elevator*. Seriously?"

"Apparently Dad insisted once Mom started talking about a game room, upstairs laundry, and a movie room." Galen straightened the bedspread and gathered up the sheets he'd just stripped and replaced. "He said it was cheaper than paying movers' medical bills and easier than trying to cart a pool table and major appliances up the front stairs anyway. It's come in handy several times. I spent six weeks using it when I busted my leg skiing, and we use it when we restock the snack bar up here or send the rugs out for cleaning."

"Ooo-oooh, fancy." Ellis laughed as Galen stuck out his tongue. "What's all the rest down that way?"

"All the gorgeous men decent?" A female voice, trained to carry either from motherhood or fucking pre-mies Broadway, filled the house. Ellis hadn't heard the front door open, so she must have come in through the mudroom he'd noticed when Ben brought his wet suit into the kitchen that first day.

Ellis watched a glow fill Galen's face, the smile not quite drying out the renewed grief behind Galen's eyes at the mention of his parents. Today might be a little tender.

"I'll go say hi, relay Joe's request about his laundry and the roses, and see what her plan is for today. She'll either be all upstairs or all downstairs this week on her cleaning spree." Galen finished setting pillows to rights and replacing the extra blanket folded at the foot of his bed. "I'd introduce you, but I honestly don't know what her reaction to a frog would be."

"No big. I'll hang."

"Back in a few, then."

Ellis shadowed Galen to the back stairs, though he stopped on the third step from the top and looked down into the kitchen from between the railing spindles.

A tall woman, who would have been slim and stunning in her prime but still held her age beautifully, smiled and opened her arms for a hug. "There's my handsome Galen. Two weeks was too long. How was Hartford?"

They chatted for a few moments. Ellis could tell just by watching them that his instincts about the earlier comments had been correct. This woman was far, far more to Galen and his brothers than simply "the help."

"I'll be here all day manning the phone and kicking back. Ben won't be home until four-ish, and Joe had to take a trip out to Kansas City to talk a client off the proverbial ledge." Galen grabbed a brownie from the box she'd just set on the counter. One bite had him groaning. "Oh God. I know I've said it about a million times by now, but I'll say it again. Molly Sheridan, you're a goddess in the kitchen."

Her wicked smile catapulted *goddess* right up to *sorceress*. "I'm still a goddess other places too."

"Yeah, yeah, tease, tease. You just know I'm safe to flirt with." The fact that Galen hadn't choked on the brownie told Ellis this conversation wasn't new, either. They seemed to feed off each other's brat-quotient. "You starting the Tornado Run upstairs or down?"

"Up. Go set your files in order so I don't accidentally knock things askew while I'm cleaning." She rolled up her sleeves, then pulled a brightly patterned kerchief from the tote she'd brought in and settled it over the dark waves of her short hair. "I'll do your office and bedroom first so you can have the space back quickly."

"I can manage to vacuum and dust my own spaces, Molly. You don't have to—" Galen laughed as she planted her hands on her hips and raised a brow at him. "All right, all right, I surrender. Stay out of your way, after thirty-five years you've got a system, I get it." He finished the last bite of brownie and wiped his mouth before kissing her cheek. "But don't you dare try moving those rugs after you get done vacuuming them. They're too heavy for you, they always have been, and there's furniture to be moved. In fact, I'm going to come move everything but beds and that pool table for you. We'll get the rest on Saturday when Joe gets back." He cut off her protest, again from long practice. "Don't argue. You know that's what needs to happen. You're just stubborn."

She smiled, softer now, and patted his cheek. "I am, and it's served me well to be so. But today I won't argue. I spent a lot of time in the garden yesterday, and my back could use a break." She waylaid the new rush of concern. "I'm fine to vacuum and dust and polish. I just could do without the heavier shoving and lifting today."

"From now on." Ellis heard Galen's voice shift, the decent stubborn streak that had risen to meet hers coupled with deeper emotions. "You'll let me or one of the other guys shove and lift and cart, and next week I'll have the plants and plates off the top of the cabinets in here before you even arrive." He hugged her again. "I want you around as long as possible."

Ellis fought the urge to just melt. *Dude, my feels cannot possibly withstand that.* If frogs possessed tear ducts, he'd have been a wreck.

"Oh, sweetheart." She ruffled Galen's hair with the familiarity of understanding how grief could pop up without warning. No doubt they'd all run a fair gauntlet of it over the past six years. "It's all right. I'm not going anywhere for a good long time yet. But if it will make you feel better, I'll take a little help." Now she pulled back enough to smile and tweak Galen's ear. "A *little*."

Galen's cheeks colored. "Sorry. Kinda hit the last couple of days."

"Grief does that now and again. But the joy does as well. And your parents were full of joy, and they raised the three of you into amazing men." Molly patted his shoulder as she stepped back. "Now, go put away your

files and then stay out of my way until I need you to
shove and lift."

Galen's grin had regained its power, and he tipped
a salute. "Yes, ma'am. Oh, Joe wanted me to tell—"

"He already texted me and offered to grovel with
roses. I told him yes and pink." She waved her hands
toward the stairs. "Now shoo."

Ellis waited until she'd left the kitchen before he
moved into Galen's view to avoid getting accidentally
kicked. "I get why you guys talk about her like she's
something special. She is."

"Yeah." Galen sighed. "Yeah, she is, and one day
she'll break my heart all over again. But not today."
He picked Ellis up and finished climbing the stairs.
"We need to go do what she told us to do and then
let her work her magic. It's sunny today, and warm
enough for you that we can hang out by the pond until
she's done."

THE pond had been the plan. Until the landline rang
just as Galen was putting away the last file.

"Townsend Consult— Oh, hi, Ms. Ryan. Joe's
not here right now, he—" Galen grabbed a pen and a
notepad, scribbling fast. "Yeah. Yeah, I can pull that
file and find what you need. Let me put you on hold
for a minute and get down to his office. Yeah, we can
Zoom if you want. It'll take me a minute to set up down
there. Sure. Okay, I'll pull the file and then buzz you in
about… fifteen minutes, okay? Got it. Yep. Talk to you
in a few minutes, then." He hung up and shrugged at
Ellis. "This could take ten minutes or an hour. You want
to come with?"

"Nah, I'm good. I think I can manage to stay out of trouble." Ellis hopped out of the paper clip tray and down from Galen's desk. "Molly was doing here and your room first, right? I'll just go find a corner of the game room to veg in."

"You can probably do a self-guided tour of the rest of this floor if you want. We've mostly hung out in my spaces. She'll have all the doors open." Galen grabbed the notepad. "I gotta go or Barb Ryan's likely to start without me. Back in a bit." He raced down the front stairs.

Ellis considered the best place to stay out of sight until he got a better idea of Molly's game plan beyond doing Galen's spaces first. He decided the counter of the game room's kitchenette would give him the widest view of the second floor. The side facing the elevator was half wall, half counter, which offered both visibility and a space to hide if needed.

He'd miscalculated that she'd come up the main stairs at the front of the house and had to duck behind a bottle of dish soap when she appeared at the back stairs instead. She turned to the right and began opening doors—and windows, he assumed, since she briefly stepped into each space before coming back out to the hall. One, two, three, four... then she crossed the hallway space and whooshed through the game room, opening the two windows that could open. A cool breeze began to work its way around and through the open expanse.

Deep hazel eyes took in the space and made quick mental note of stuff that needed doing. Ellis felt a grin tickle its way through his nervous system. *Go, General Sheridan. No wonder Galen stays out of her way.* He peeked around the wall once she went out around the length of the kitchenette counter to enter Galen's bedroom and office.

She came out of the office space doorway at the end of the hall, and Ellis braced to duck again as she came back to either the rear stairs or the elevator to go get her cleaning supplies. Instead, she opened a door he hadn't noticed before, situated between Galen's office and the front stairs. *Ohhh yeah, Galen mentioned that.* An upstairs laundry room, complete with a ruthlessly organized set of shelves holding cleaning supplies and a cart she began to load with what she needed.

Okay, she'd be a little while in Galen's space, so his best course of curiosity was to start at the opposite end. He waited until she and her cart were in Galen's office, then hopped down from the counter and across the thirty-ish feet to where the hall space ended beyond the back stairs.

Wow. If Ben wasn't looking for company tonight, Ellis was calling Movie Night with Galen. Hell, maybe even if Ben did want to hang with them. "Roland" could easily show up again.

On his right, a cinema-style television dominated one wall of a paneled room. A sectional sofa and a well-worn coffee table invited kicking back, and a small alcove behind the sofa boasted built-in cabinets and a counter for a popcorn popper with a mini-fridge below. At the far end of the room, a dormer alcove held an audio system and a serious vinyl collection. Dual chairs and dual headphones sat ready. Framed albums and vintage tin signs made the space unabashedly male.

Oh yeah, serious vinyl. The records were too heavy for him to thumb through as a frog, but what he could read of the jacket edges told him plenty.

Someone was into vintage blues. While Ellis didn't listen to it much himself, he recognized names from his father's collection. Muddy Waters, Bessie Smith, Paul Butterfield... wow, even a Blind Blake album Ellis suspected had come at a hell of a price. Galen hadn't played blues at all while they'd been together, so they likely weren't his go-to. He didn't know the other Townsend brothers, but if he had to wager on one based on first impressions alone, he'd guess Ben. The sudden mental flash of Mr. Almost-PhD Finance sitting lotus-style in one of the chairs or on the floor, soaking in delta blues like a psychic bubble bath, left Ellis chuckling.

Classic rock filled out most of the remaining titles, along with an occasional album in folk, Celtic, punk, or jazz. The headphones were high-end, the chairs designed to offer the sensation of floating while you were listening. *Nice.*

He came back out to the hallway. Since Molly hadn't opened the single door in the corner, Ellis assumed it was likely a closet of some sort. The double doors to the left of it looked far more interesting.

This must have been Joe's room when they were kids. Ellis suspected it had undergone some major remodeling when the brothers turned it into a guest suite, but there was certainly enough room for a young boy to hoard his private toys and treasures and for a teenager to sprawl out. Now it offered cool mint-green walls and hardwood in spades, from the pale floorboards to the darker furniture and doors. A built-in window seat complemented the loveseat and small television, a curved corner desk provided workspace, and the entire room exuded a casual elegance to rival any high-end

hotel. The ensuite bath was just as impressive. They'd
even installed a steam shower.

He realized he'd spent more time than he'd intended
in the generous space—or seriously misjudged her
cleaning speed—when he heard the roar of a vacuum
cleaner coming closer. He hopped back to the doorway
and peeked around the open door.

Oh shit. Not just any vacuum. Ellis recognized
this behemoth from the summer stock company's
theater, though from his current height it looked
like a goddamn jumbo jet. An industrial-suction
bagged vacuum monogrammed "The Pig" by its
manufacturer, designed to immediately pick up just
about anything that would fit through its nozzle.
He'd seen the one at the theater inhale popcorn,
squashed Airheads stuck on the carpet, and any
costume piece or small prop carelessly left lying on
the floor. *Nothing* recovered from being Pigged. The
damn thing had been known to actually lift or drag
set pieces if the person operating it wasn't paying
attention.

And as a four-inch frog, *he* more than qualified as
the "anything" the Pig would eat. If he got within eight
inches of that maw and wasn't fortunate enough to
meet it head-on, the suction on the damn thing would
rip him apart before depositing him in a dark pile of
debris. Even a head-on collision would likely give
him multiple concussions and suck out his eardrums
before he landed in a moisture-leaching dust-fest.
Between the noise and whatever Molly had going
in her headphones, even if he managed a scream—
human or frog—she wouldn't hear him in time to
prevent a rapid and grisly death or a slow desiccation.
Galen would likely search the house for him first, and

even then might not think of the vacuum until rescue would be way, way too late.

No, no, no, I am not getting this close to breaking the damn spell only to buy it now. And he sure as hell didn't want to give Galen another reason to grieve.

His hopes of her hitting the first room she came to vanished, and he ducked back behind the guest suite door as the floor attachment hugged the edge of the hallway. She paused, covering every inch of the hallway's end, and for one moment he thought for sure she'd go into the media room first and allow him time to escape around this door and back to Galen's room. And he would have to go *around* the door; the space between the frame and the hinges was too small even for him.

Instead, she chose to vacuum the two large rugs in the hallway, where he would be in her view the moment he moved. He'd noted the next door down led to a small powder room, a tiny thing that would offer zero cover. The double doors beyond that he hadn't paid much attention to, but he thought there might have been books. He'd have to cross the hallway to get back to Galen's space, leaving him equally vulnerable to the vacuum if Molly was the freakout sort when it came to small amphibians.

So he sat, heart hammering, while she finished. Even when the vacuum was off and she bent to roll up the two rugs—he noted she didn't try to shift them beyond that—he'd scare the hell out of her if he moved. Then the Pig roared back to life, and she stepped into the guest suite instead of the media room.

Oh God, oh God, oh shit. If she did the entrance first, he was a dead frog. If she went to the back of the room first, he *might* be able to sneak out around the door. Going back into the room himself wasn't an option; she'd vacuum under the bed and the other furniture without looking, raising the odds of that grisly dismemberment to DEFCON 1. Hiding in the bathroom would be equally suicidal. *Do the back of the room first, nice lady, please....*

He peered through the small crack under the door and tried his damnedest to not shit himself as the vacuum attachment roared a mere inch away, the floor brush thing keeping most of the suction away from him, all of it looking like a bulldozer from his height. Not for the first time, Ellis felt like he'd been trapped in *Honey, I Shrunk the Kids*. Molly's sneaker was the size of a sedan.

Thank God for double doors. And that she started behind the one he wasn't using for cover. But both the warning and the game plan—she'd taken the floor brush off in order to get the corners—left him shaking. He had about sixty seconds before that maw landed right where he was sitting.

What do I do, what do I do— Wait. He glanced back into the room and noticed the small accent table placed just beyond the door's swing radius. Set there as a place for keys and sunglasses, it had a lower shelf. If he could make it in one jump, he could hide behind the decorative basket set there until Molly finished her corner sweep, then escape when she moved farther into the room.

But a single leap without smacking his head on the upper part of the table.... That was going to take some finesse he wasn't sure he had time to come up with. Then the door she was working at bumped the wall and finesse took a header as he leapt toward the table with visions of cartoon splats racing in his brain, clearing the floorspace just as that damn nozzle landed where he'd been sitting. He tumbled onto the edge of the basket, teetered there for what felt like a week, then managed to get his balance enough to avoid having to crawl out of it along with everything else.

Okay, okay, just breathe, you're good, you're all good. He could feel the Pig sucking air even though he was out of range. It didn't help his nerves, especially when Molly slid the table away from the wall to vacuum under it. His overloaded brain blanked except for a mental chant of *just keep breathing, just keep breathing, just keep breathing* in Ellen DeGeneres's voice.

Finally the table settled back into place and Molly led the Pig farther into the room. Ellis didn't even wait for Ellen to quit chanting before he careened out of the suite and across the hall, parkouring off the cleaning cart and whatever furniture was in his path like a sentient ping-pong ball. Only when he reached his makeshift pool on Galen's nightstand did he stop, muscles vibrating, heart racing, adrenaline making even the water against his skin hurt.

It's okay, it's okay, it's okay.... He slumped onto the bowl "rock." *Goddamn Pig. Had to be a goddamn Pig.* Lightheaded, mouth dry, he offered gratitude to all the deities he could immediately think of, and a few more as his brain began to work properly again. Then to the overall universe just to accentuate his level of relief.

"Hey. Sorry that took so long." Galen sauntered back into the room and dropped the notepad on the bed. "What'd I miss?"

"Oh, nothing." Ellis hoped he could manage to catch his breath before the truth came out.

OH, oh God...." Galen held his sides, laughter rolling out over the lawn.

Ellis leveled a glare at him from the pond wall. *Brat.*

Still, he supposed there was humor in it, now that the Pig was safely corralled in the laundry room and no actual carnage had taken place. The afternoon sun bathed everything in a golden glow, the woods ramping up their fall colors and the lily pads starting to yellow at the edges. Ellis doubted the orange flowers would last much longer; there was a frost forecast for tonight. Thank God he had winter digs worked out.

"Molly's going to wonder what you're smoking, you keep this up." He glanced up at the open doors along the first floor. "Thought she was only doing upstairs today."

"She is." Galen managed to suck in a breath. "She's just finishing up Joe's wash, but she takes any chance she gets to just air everything out. Ben texted while I was on the Skype with Barb Ryan. He's hit a groove on his dissertation and will stay until the library closes, so we can... bounce around the place by ourselves until about ten." The poorly controlled snicker became a new round of helpless laughter.

"At 9:01 tonight I'm taking you over my knee." That visual made it hard to stay annoyed, but he could still pout—more or less. "You try facing down a two-story reverse wind tunnel on high without shitting yourself and see how funny it is."

"I know, I know, I'm sorry...." Galen did seem to be making an effort to get himself under control. "It's just...

the whole parkour thing... I can picture... this little green dot all over the place.... Oh God...." He wiped at his streaming eyes with his sleeve. "Oh shit...."

"Galen, what on earth are you laughing at?" Molly approached the pond, a smile lighting her face. "Sitting out here all by yourself bursting a seam. Are you okay?"

"Yeah, I'm okay, Molly, sorry." Galen pulled in a full breath for the first time in what seemed to Ellis like an hour. "I just... I...." He hid the obvious-to-Ellis and frantic search for an explanation behind another breath.

"Read a tweet?" Ellis offered, keeping his voice low enough to not carry beyond the lounge.

Galen nodded and picked up his phone from where it had fallen from his shirt pocket onto the grass. "Just something somebody tweeted. It hit the funny bone hard, that's all." He muffled another snicker. "You done for the day?"

"I am. I'm going home and bury myself in a good mystery story before dinner." She ruffled Galen's hair. "If you're breathing again."

"Yeah, I'm good."

"Good." And suddenly she noticed Ellis. "Well, hello there."

It took every effort to not reply. Since she hadn't screamed and seemed perfectly content to converse with the wildlife, he found it equally difficult to behave like a wild frog and actually flinch when she picked him up.

"Oh, he's a handsome one." She took in Galen's tension with a smile. "I used to chase frogs and salamanders when I was a girl. We lived near a river like the Bungay here. All summer we'd drive my mother

crazy with dragonflies and butterflies and tadpoles."
She set Ellis back on the wall. "Odd, though, to see one
this late in the season."

Galen swallowed once. "Um...."

"I'm sure he'll find a spot to hibernate shortly. The
nights are getting far too chilly." She patted Galen's
shoulder. "I'll see you next week, then. Wednesday,
nine sharp. We'll shove some more furniture around."

"Absolutely." Galen got up to give her a hug. "And
Joe will bring your roses over when he gets home."

"He'd better." She winked at Galen and headed
back toward the house.

Ellis waited until she was out of earshot. "Yep.
She's something special."

Chapter Eight

GALEN stretched and yawned his way awake at seven thirty on Friday morning to find Ellis curled beside him, pale blond strands in his face, long body warm and smooth and human. *Dear God, he's perfect.* He slipped his arms around the sleeping figure, drawing close, easing Ellis's head to his shoulder, letting his hands slide over satiny skin.

The soft groan caught him low in his gut, enough that he pulled Ellis's hips even closer, feeling arousal to match his own. Probably didn't have time for everything, but they could still play a little. Galen smiled as he ground slowly against Ellis, watching one narrow eyebrow rise over a sleepy green gaze.

"Mmh… time is it?" God, even Ellis's voice with its low rumble followed by a little squeak wound Galen a little tighter.

He applied a love bite to a slim throat. "Half past seven. We have a few minutes if the pattern holds. It has so far." Years of waking up like this warmed his thoughts. He slipped one hand between them, capturing their erections together. "Let me make you feel good. I like watching you when you feel good."

"Fuck…." Ellis tipped his head back, one hand gripping Galen's bicep and the other trapped beneath them but cupping the curve of Galen's ass. "Yeah…."

Having to keep one eye on the clock killed the mood a bit, but only a bit. Forcing Ellis to slow down, to just feel, focused Galen's attention. He grinned at the curse he got for massaging Ellis's tip with unrelenting slowness. His own desire ached, but it would wait… one… minute… more….

"God!" Ellis surged against him, liquid heat between them enough to send Galen over the edge as well. Ellis panted, limp in Galen's arms, voice rough against Galen's shoulder. "You are too damn good at that. You really are."

"Breathe." Galen held him close, stroking both hair and skin. "Get your bearings. It's likely only a few minutes now." He resisted Ellis's push away. "No. You're staying right here. You're not hiding from me anymore, do you understand?"

"But—"

"I mean it. I don't care if you're still mid-spell. Human or frog, you're staying right here with me, and you're not hiding anything." He cradled high cheekbones and pressed a kiss to Ellis's lips as the hall clock began to strike. "Look at me."

He wasn't sure what he'd expected. Ellis had described a feeling of being pulled down a dark funnel, narrower with each second. And that did pretty much cover it. No sparkles, no puff of smoke, no sound, just a bit of… melting… around the edges as Ellis stiffened and was… the best term Galen could think of at the moment, thanks to a childhood filled with fairy tales and Disney movies, was a man-shaped genie being sucked down into a frog-shaped lamp in the space of about three seconds. The smoothest CGI Hollywood could have ever created. There didn't seem to be any discomfort to it; Ellis had never said it hurt. The million engineering questions started up again in his brain, but he decided to file those away. Just amazing, though.

Ellis shook off one webbed foot when Galen pulled back the covers. "Thinking a shower might be a good idea for us both. This'll seriously fuck up the terrarium."

Laughter took no effort. "Done. There's a decent shelf you can hang out on while I soap up, since the last thing we want is to dry you out or poison you."

"View might finish me off, though… pretty boy." Golden eyes favored Galen with unabashed warmth. "Thank you. For seeing me. I— "

"We're a team, remember?" Galen gathered up the bedding for a trip to the washer. *And I love you.*

If only he dared say it aloud. But he didn't know if Ellis would want to continue a relationship once the spell broke, or even if it didn't. If the spell broke, would he be a constant reminder of what Ellis had been through? If the spell *never* broke, would the depression get to be too much for Ellis to deal with? He'd already tried once to— Would Ellis decide to go home and spend the rest of his life as a frog near his parents?

Confessing his love meant Galen's heart would be gone, and he had no idea if it would recover when Ellis inevitably left.

FRIDAY night. Hard to believe it had been a week since Galen's life took a serious turn into the Twilight Zone. Hard to believe he'd known Ellis for *only* a week.

Joe had returned from his business trip just a couple hours ago and was still in his room, no doubt racing through a shower. Galen watched Ben fuss with his tie in the mirror over the bar in the parlor. "Don't you guys ever go anywhere casual anymore?"

"Image is everything. You know that." His brother tempered the snotty tone with a smile. "Townsend means class. Or so the chat rooms say. Wonder what the set would do if they knew I lurk every chance I get. Probably all faint into their appletinis." A last twitch of the tie and tug on the cufflinks. "You got plans tonight other than reading? That guy Roland seemed nice."

"Yeah, he might drop by." Galen left it at that.

"Good. You seem happier this week." Ben turned from the parlor mirror and hollered down the hall. "Joseph! Let's go!"

"In a sec." Joe's voice filtered down the back stairs.

Wait. Down the stairs? *But his suite's on the first floor now....*

"Hey, Galen, I'm borrowing your—" A blood-chilling scream and a sudden crash interrupted everything.

Galen raced up the front stairs, realizing he'd actually started moving before Joe had even finished "borrowing." *Shit, shit, shit, he went into my room and found....* Ben stampeded right on his heels.

As feared, the baking dish was a mess of glass and water on his floor and Joe stood in the middle of Galen's bedroom, lacrosse stick wielded like an axe, face sheet-pale, glaring under the nightstand. Ellis cowered beneath it; Galen could see one tiny foot sticking out.

Ben came in behind. "Joe, what the ever-loving—"

"A frog! A goddamned fucking frog!" Joe kicked the nightstand aside and, before Galen could stop him, swept Ellis up in the net portion of the lacrosse stick. He stalked to the balcony. "Let's see what the little fucker looks like splattered all over Italian tile."

"No!" Galen grabbed at the stick, wrestling Joe for it, trying to at least keep it over the balcony and not suspended over the very *hard* Italian tile ten feet below. "Joe, for Christ's sake!"

Fortunately, Ellis stayed tangled in the open weave, no doubt clinging on for dear life.

"Let go, will you?" Galen tugged at the stick again. "God, I've got him, all right? Take a fucking breath already. He's mine."

Joe's face darkened from the pale it had just been. "What do you mean, he's yours? You've got a fucking frog for a pet? What the hell? You know I hate those things!"

"He's not hopping around the house! He stays in my room!" Galen tried to get a better grip on the lacrosse stick and keep an eye on Ellis at the same time. "That's what you get for wandering in here without permission!"

His brother's voice broke between deep gulping breaths. "Since when... do we need... fucking permission... to enter a room in this house! We've never done that shit!" He yanked on the stick again, visibly shaking. "You could have at least... *said* you got a frog!"

Galen wasn't much steadier. "If I had, you'd have freaked out in the first ten seconds!" Obvious, that. "Now *let go*!"

Finally, after what felt like a fair portion of Galen's life and certainly most of his wits, Joe let go of the stick and backed up against a wall, color drained again and the shaking no better. "G-get that thing out of here! Get it out!"

"Joe, what the fuck?" Ben pinched the bridge of his nose, looking two seconds from rolling his eyes. "It's just a frog. Jesus Christ. It's been what, twenty years now?"

"You're the one who dumped a toad down his trunks at Lacey Pond when I was seven! You scarred him for life." Galen untangled the net and tucked Ellis into his shirt pocket. "Joe, stay the hell out of my room if you don't want to see him. What the fuck were you wanting to borrow, anyway?"

"I don't remember now. Never mind." Joe stomped off down the front stairs, still muttering phrases their mother would never have allowed in the house while she was alive.

Ben glanced after him. "He'll cool down once he gets a couple drinks in him. I hadn't realized it was still that bad."

"Yeah, well, you work it out with him, because I'm not getting rid of—" Hmm... saying Ellis's name or surname was likely a bad idea, as Ben was the one who'd found the designer suit that first day. "Roland" wasn't going to work. And anything off-the-cuff would take more brain cells than he currently had to spare after the terror of a moment ago; he could still feel his heart racing and had to fight to not let his trembling show. So Galen served up a shrug instead. "Still working on a name."

"Let's see him." Ben smiled as Galen fished Ellis out of his pocket. He considered the frog a moment, brows drawn together in thought. "Suppose you could go for the obvious and spell 'frog' backwards."

"Gorf?" The utterly insulted expression on Ellis's face, though Ben probably couldn't pick out the nuances, nearly demolished Galen's tentative control into hysterical laughter. He swallowed hard before he could speak. "This is why Joe does the marketing. I'll think up something. You better get going before Joe tries to drive in Freakout Mode." Or before Ellis morphed right in front of him. Galen really couldn't take *another* freakout right now.

Ben checked his watch. "Yeah, it's nearly nine. The ladies are waiting." He turned and headed for the stairs. "I'll check in with you when I get home tomorrow. You might want to consider a better terrarium for Gorf, though. One he can't get out of." A smirk lit the entire space at Galen's glare. "Hey, say it often enough, it'll stick. Later."

Ellis waited until Ben was out of earshot before snorting. "Yep. Definitely kicking his ass if I ever get out of this shitstorm."

Galen cradled Ellis closer in his hand, heart still hammering. "Are you okay? Did he hit you? Was I too rough getting you out of the net? Are you—"

"Easy, sport." Tiny webbed toes smoothed across his palm. "I'm okay. It's okay."

"God…." He had to sit before he passed out from relief. The memory foam of his bed caught him. He let Ellis tumble to the blanket and allowed himself to fall the rest of the way, staring up at the ceiling. "I thought…. God, I thought I was going to lose you."

"I'm right here." Soft and low in his ear, cool touch to his cheek. "I'm right here, Galen. It's okay."

"I can't lose you. I love you." He heard the clock in the hall chime the hour and reached out, eyes closed, for Ellis. "I love you."

Strong arms caught him, held him. Long legs tangled with his. "It's okay, Galen. We're okay."

"No we're not." The images of Ellis flying off the edge of the balcony wouldn't stop. *I can fix this. I have to fix this.* "He'll be gunning for you every minute. A terrarium won't stop him." Galen pushed up off the bed, stalked to his desk, and brought the computer out of idle. "I should have done this days ago. I figured with the Gyro engine and then everything else…. But I should have made time." He shot a look at Ellis. "Tell me exactly what happened with Wayne."

Ellis's brows popped up, probably at the anger and near-terror Galen wasn't ready to let go of just yet. "What are you going to do, look up *www.Warlocks-R-Us.com*? I already tried… well, I tried searching for *turned into a frog* and got nothing but Disney movies and Final Fantasy gameplay tips."

"I'm a goddamned engineer. It's a puzzle, just like any other puzzle." *I can fix this.* Goddammit, he'd taken apart that fucking motor and put it back together properly—and it wasn't even the most complex prototype he'd ever worked on. He'd fixed production plans and timelines and thirty-person-design-team fuckups. It was all in the moving parts. A magick spell couldn't be that much different. "Let's start at the start. How'd you hook up with him in the first place?"

"Galen, it's not really—"

"Tell me." He wasn't going to be able to stop shaking until he at least tried to figure it out.

Ellis sighed and got up, moving to carefully gather the glass bits of the smashed baking dish and put them in the bowl that had survived. "One of my mom's horse shows about a year and a half ago. We met back in the parking area." He stepped into the bathroom and came out with a towel, laying it over the now glass-free puddle on the wood floor. "We were bored out of our skulls and decided to just hang out together until the competition was done."

"I suspect you ended up doing more than hanging out?" The twinge of jealousy was just an extension of his current anger at the world in general, Galen knew, but it still simmered in his gut.

"Talking, figuring out we were both interested and consenting, little kissing, little groping. Needless to say, the horses got something extra in their trailer bedding I'd just finished laying out." More glass shards from under the bed went into the bowl. "Given what I'd cleaned out of it earlier, I wasn't feeling overly guilty." Ellis read Galen's reaction too well and a smirk curved his lips. "Told you the mojo is strong with this one."

He refused to allow his teeth to actually grind. That visual, even though Galen had no physical description of Wayne, plastered itself onto the back of his brain. "Stayed in touch, then." Shit, that really wasn't supposed to come out with a heavy dash of bitter or minus the question mark.

"The phone sex was pretty damn good too." Ellis finally got up and came over to kiss Galen's cheek from behind, arms wrapping Galen's waist. "But that's all it was. It was okay, but it never really went past sex.

Good enough sex to plan a weekend romp at his place in New York, though." He rubbed his cheek against Galen's. "Nothing like this with you. I swear."

"I'm assuming you took the train down." While he appreciated Ellis's attempt at calming, he wasn't ready for calm yet and the tension hardened his voice.

A new sigh tickled his ear and the embrace tightened. "Yes. He suggested his place because I still live with my folks and his work might call. He told me he was an analytical chemist. Never occurred to me 'analytical' might mean 'warlock' instead."

Galen *hmphed* a brief agreement with that. "So what happened?"

"I'd barely dropped my bag in the entry when he had me in a lip-lock and almost ripped my polo shirt off. It wasn't thirty seconds before we were naked on the couch and he's sucking my dick like he's a fucking Electrolux. Tongue, teeth, the works. Plus he's got my balls in one hand and my prostate at the tips of the other. World went up in a fireball for… I don't know how long. I didn't even notice the simmering pots and the candles and shit until after, and then I just figured he was setting the mood. For all I know, he spit my spunk into a cauldron while I was still trying to breathe properly again."

"So a potion most likely." Galen realized he was bordering on rude, but his brain wouldn't let go of the vision of Joe dropping Ellis over the balcony or Wayne essentially molesting Ellis. He *had* to figure this out if he could. He typed *transfiguration potion* into the browser. When that netted nothing more than Halloween décor and a blogger who clearly led a rich fantasy life but didn't appear to be an actual practicing witch, he decided he needed a little more information. "You said polo shirt. You left a suit out in the gazebo."

Ellis chuckled. "Nice catch, CSI."

"Did he curse you or whatever right after the blow job?"

Another sigh. "No. Though now that I think about it, he did seem to be watching me for some sort of… reaction, I guess, all through the nice dinner we went out for afterward. And the flat smelled kind of like licorice and roses." Ellis paused. "And… cloves, I think. I'd figured it was some weird-ass potpourri."

Galen tried *licorice cloves rose spell* and got some hits for spell work, though nothing combining them all. "Looks like they're all used in love and lust spells, and it's mentioned on a Pinterest post about obsession magick."

"That tracks. I remember him telling me when we first met that he wanted someone to stick around, that his other dates just hadn't understood him. I mean, I'd figured it was just the Goth makeup and the… I think it's called a pentacle… pendant, a little too into his cosplay, you know." Ellis apparently decided he wasn't going to tease or seduce Galen out of the research right away and moved to the small sofa used as a dressing space in front of Galen's closet. "So he was, what, trying to magick me into sticking around?"

"And looking for signs of whether it was working." Galen tried another site. "Hmm… says here love spells depend not only on the proficiency of the one casting it, but also the resolve of *both* the… participants…. I'm guessing you weren't being sufficiently obsessive."

Ellis snorted. "Yeah, you could say that. Especially when we got back to the flat and he's like 'Wanna see something cool?' Dude drew one of those pentacles on the floor, then sets out candles and lights them *without touching them*. That was the point where I'm like, 'Okaaay. Um, maybe the sex isn't great enough for, you know, *this*. I think maybe I'll find a hotel and catch the early train tomorrow.' Pulled out my cellphone, and that's when he whammied me."

"What exactly did he do?" Galen cracked his knuckles in preparation for more typing... or punching worthless prick warlocks in the teeth at first sight. "If we can recreate it, we can maybe figure out how to undo it."

The look Ellis gave him held something unreadable, but soft and warm enough to put the tiniest chink in Galen's dark mood. "You're sitting here dead serious that you can undo black magick with your engineering skills. That's got to be either the most adorable thing I've ever witnessed or the most insane. Probably both."

"You pulled out your phone to find a hotel." If he stopped now he'd likely still break into a million pieces for the rest of the evening. "Then what?"

"He grabbed my pocket scarf and dragged it across my lips, threw it into the bigger pot that was still simmering, and shouted something in... could have been Latin, could have been Martian for all I know. There's this huge puff of deep purple smoke, and suddenly I'm looking up at him from six inches off the ground." Ellis seemed to pull into himself at the memory, crossing his arms over his chest and scowling. "I have a very good reference point if I ever decide to do Jack and that goddamn beanstalk at a community theater."

Galen made a few notes on a pad next to his computer. "And you're pretty sure it was black magick he used? I saw something in the first search called white magick as well."

"Not a clue. Wayne didn't tell me shit about the spell itself. Just stood there with a smirk on his face, telling me no one would look twice at a frog in a tank on his bookshelf, that he'd keep me there and change me back whenever he got an urge for sex. Fortunately, he'd left a window cracked and the fire escape was right there. Bit of a chase similar to the Great Vacuum Incident." Ellis thought for a moment. "I'd guess black magick, though, given the décor of the place and jars labeled with names other than chamomile and peppermint. Half of them looked like something out of *Hellraiser*. I seriously thought they were just for decoration."

"Okay. That's our place to start." Someone somewhere had to have a blog or website about it. He began searching. "So if this is black magick rather than white... oh shit, there's red magick as well? Never heard of that, but... hmm, here's a ritual to block curses." He scanned down over the post. "This calls for moon water. What the hell is— Oh, wait, there's a link...."

Ellis got back up and peered over his shoulder at the screen. "I've heard stuff about charging crystals under a full moon. Maybe something similar, only with water?"

"Yeah, yeah, that's what they're talking about here. Oh wait... 'Keep in mind the astrological sign the moon is in while making moon water. For example, a waxing moon in Taurus will carry different properties than moon water made under a waning moon in Pisces, etc.'" Galen tabbed back and forth between the ritual and the links to the various ingredients, all of which had to be gathered or charged or cleansed in just the right way at just the right time under just the right circumstances. "Oh my God, this is worse than my Environmental Regulations class…." He read to the bottom of the original post. "Goddammit, this isn't even the right recipe. It won't reverse something already cast, it's just for protection." He growled at the screen. "All right, we'll start over. What did—"

Ellis removed Galen's hand from the mouse and swiveled him around on the stool. "Galen. Stop. You're going to research yourself into a straightjacket."

"I can do it. It's just another puzzle. It's…." No, he couldn't stop. If he stopped Ellis would turn back into a frog and Joe would find him and— He swallowed against tears and gave up trying to hold back the shakes, leaning his head against Ellis's chest. "It's just another puzzle…."

"You can't become a master wizard in an afternoon. Even if it doesn't require a natural talent or whatever for it." Warm lips pressed into his hair. "But thank you for trying."

"I can't lose you, Ellis. I can't lose you too." Galen wrapped his arms tight around Ellis's waist, breathing in the scent of his lover.

"You're not going to lose me." More kisses in his hair. "I can stay out of Joe's sight now that I know the level of freakout we're dealing with. If you want to start studying this stuff, there's time for you to do it without wrecking yourself in the process. We're okay, babe. We're really okay." Strong arms pulled him to his feet. "Come back to the bed. We'll curl up together until you can breathe again."

How long they stayed there, cuddled together, kissing, Galen wasn't sure and didn't care until

Ellis's stomach let out a loud growl. He unwound his tongue from his lover's and murmured against the smooth curve of collarbone. "Suppose we ought to get something to eat."

Soft laughter tickled his ear. "If I thought I'd stay human this time, I have an idea or two about that." Mischievous fingers trailed up Galen's fly. "But yeah, we probably should. Delivery and a movie sound okay? I don't feel like going back out into the world, even long enough for dinner. That thing with Dena was too close for comfort."

"Staying in sounds perfect. Pet store isn't open this late anyway. Ben's right, though. If you're staying the winter, we'd better set something up so Joe isn't trying to kill you every other day." Galen managed to get to his feet and over to the desk, then found he still had to have Ellis right with him even for something as simple as a Web delivery order. "I know you're okay, but my insides are still shaking."

Ellis grinned as he settled cool hands on Galen's shoulders. "You planning to follow me into the shower too? Can't say as I'd complain."

Now there was a plan. Galen checked the confirmation and dropped his reading glasses back on the wood surface. "We've got twenty minutes."

"CAN I just say, I really like this design." Ellis lit a couple of candles on the shelf above the deep tub and slipped his boxers off. "We're gonna have to come play here some evening when the doorbell's not going to ring."

"Oh God, that sounds incredible. Or in the sauna downstairs. But not tonight. I have a different idea, since we already agreed we're not going to go full-on right now." Galen had already shed his clothes and dropped them in the hamper on the other side of the divider shelf. He took Ellis's hand and led them into the shower, turning the water on and adjusting the temperature. "Come get wet with me."

"Wet in the shower? How's that different?" Ellis was glad Galen had stopped shaking, but he wondered exactly what his lover had in mind and if it was something residual from the close call. He pulled Galen tight against him. "No complaints, though. You feel as good as ever."

"Just wait. And let go of me a second. You have to be completely wet for this to work."

Oookay. Not entirely sure of the direction here, but Ellis was willing to follow. He made use of a hand-held sprayer that supplemented the rain shower overhead. A grin curled his lips as he let his gaze wander down over Galen's form. "Completely, huh?"

"Completely." Lord, the intensity in those blue eyes sent a shiver up Ellis's spine. Long fingers removed the sprayer from his grasp and aimed it so warm water flowed over Ellis's hardening shaft and then under to catch his balls and farther to stream up between his asscheeks. Galen completed the journey over the non-erotic areas of Ellis's body, then doused himself before turning the water off and reaching for a bottle on the shower shelf. "You have any kind of soap allergy?"

Ellis had to take a breath before he could reply, his skin tingling from the sensation of the water jet. "Not as a human. What exactly are we doing, sport? We don't have much more time than it takes to soap up and rinse off, unless you plan to open the front door like this." Now his breathless feeling was all for the image that comment plastered on the back of his brain. "God, you'd look incredible."

Galen squeezed a generous line of pale blue soap across his own chest at nipple level and another across his navel. "I know we don't have much time. I figured we could soap up together." He moved close again, pressing Ellis against the tile wall, sliding over Ellis's chest and abdomen, shifting up and down, side to side, until they were both lathered and Ellis moaned at the sensation. "How's that feel?"

"Oh my God, where did you learn that?" Even the slight chill of the bathroom air on his wet skin couldn't dull that feeling, especially when Galen turned him around and did the exact same move over Ellis's back and ass. Another squeeze of shower gel across lean thighs that rubbed over his and between them and a knee gliding up to slide against his balls and the bottom of his ass crack. "Shit, I don't care. Just keep doing it."

The rich chuckle in his ear sounded so much better than the squeaky, near breaking point laugh of a few minutes ago. A quick douse of water to warm them up without washing away too much soap, and then Galen turned him around again and kissed him deeply while slowly grinding against him from nipples to crotch. The silky friction had Ellis's dick wide-awake and tucked into the narrow space under Galen's hip joint, an equally hard shaft tucked against his own.

"I love you." Galen pulled back just enough that Ellis could see those beautiful eyes without losing even an inch of their bodies touching. "It wasn't just because I was terrified Joe was going to throw you off the balcony. I felt it coming before now, but I was afraid to say it because it's only been a week, and we've got no fucking idea what's going to happen today, tomorrow, or whenever. But it's true. And when I saw you in that net, hanging on for dear life, I knew that frog or man or days or months or years, I love you and I had to tell you." The slide of skin on skin slowed even further, but the strokes lengthened and Galen's hands joined in to cup low under the curves of Ellis's ass, fingers reaching farther to stroke the sensitive area behind his sac. "I always want us to feel like this. And I really, really hope you feel the same, because I'm going to feel like a complete jackass if you don't."

If I don't? Seriously. Ellis pushed into Galen's touch and let a kiss say what he couldn't form words for at the moment. He collected a handful of suds and slid his fingers up into Galen's hair, around Galen's ears, then in slow circles down the length of Galen's spine, all the while tangling his tongue with Galen's, exploring every corner of that luscious mouth. Years of this, decades, a lifetime…. It was so easy to fall into that picture.

He realized when Galen tried to pull back that he'd stayed silent too long and had probably triggered some new fear. He brought his hands up over Galen's ribs to catch the other man under the arms and hold on, teasing his thumbs over Galen's nipples and watching his lover's eyes roll back and a delightful gasp catch on parted lips. Ellis turned them around to press Galen against the wall and reached to turn the rain shower head back on. As the soap began to run down into the drain, he settled his tongue in the hollow of Galen's throat for a moment before looking up into sky-blue eyes. "Yes, I feel the same. I love you too. I didn't say it back there on the bed simply because you looked like you were going to pass out and then we got caught up trying to reverse-engineer a spell." He reached for the bottle again and poured a little more shower gel, lathering Galen's hair properly this time and then making sure it was rinsed fully while he eased their bodies apart bit by bit and slowly cooled the water so they could recover somewhat from their hard-ons before one of them answered the door for dinner. Galen's fingers in his own hair felt like… home. "I don't know what's ahead, but I know that. I love you."

The words didn't come again until much later, after dinner in the kitchen and a couple hours of darts and pool in the game room. Curled together in bed, skin to skin and drowsily warm, Galen sighed against Ellis's shoulder. "Love you."

Screw the fucking spell. He had this, would always have this. Ellis pressed a kiss to Galen's temple and cuddled closer. "I love you too, Galen." And tomorrow morning before he morphed back to a frog, he'd show Galen fully just how much. They had each other. It was enough. Ellis grinned. "Frog down the pants, huh? I might have to try that in the morning. That whole close-up tongue thing."

That whimper was more than enough, too.

Chapter Nine

ELLIS stretched, curling into the warmth of the blankets and the sun shining into the bedroom. He reached over to pull Galen close, fully intending to work his way down over that tight form until he could get his mouth around a long, delicious morning snack, and found only cool sheets.

Huh? Bathroom, probably. They'd talked and cuddled and played pool and had pizza and watched… something cute and sexy he couldn't remember now because he'd been far more interested in Galen… until nearly 4:00 a.m., then fallen asleep in each other's arms.

His own system demanded getting up to use the bathroom, and he was surprised to find the facilities empty. So Galen wasn't here either.

Maybe something for work. Last-minute calls were surely a common thing even on a Saturday, with the sort of business the Townsend brothers had going. Or more fallout with Joe from Amphibigeddon the night before. He'd get cleaned up and settled before his inevitable morph back into frogdom. The new baking dish that had replaced the broken one still had plenty of water.

The quick shower—since they hadn't done much to get dirty again after last night—felt marvelous, the towel more so. Shaving became an adventure in sensation; he'd barely noticed it just after he'd first morphed back to human, and even before the spell had been able to go a few days before stubble was even noticeable. So now it was new and amazing, and he couldn't believe he'd taken it for granted before.

"Ellis?"

Galen's voice pulled him from his thoughts. Ellis tossed the towel into the hamper and walked naked out into the bedroom. "You're up early. I was planning to wake you up in the most erotic way I could think of, and you were already gone. What'd you do, go out for donuts?"

He'd figured on a raised brow at his playful exhibitionism and the erotic wake-up offer—but was unprepared for the utterly shocked expression on Galen's face, eyes like plates, mouth open and slack. "What?" He swung to make sure he wasn't dragging toilet paper or some other mortifying thing. Turning back met the same astonishment. "Galen, *what*?"

"It's noon."

"Well, we were up pretty late. You said you didn't have anything on the board, so what's wrong with sleeping in? I certainly have no problem cuddling with you every second we can get in." He closed the distance between them, reaching out to touch Galen's elbow, wondering why his simple explanation didn't seem to have helped things. "What?"

"Ellis, it's *noon*. Yesterday you were a frog again at *eight*." Galen's eyes stayed wide even as his mouth recovered. He barely managed to set a stack of several boxes down on his desk chair.

Eight? Noon? He hadn't been paying attention. The clock didn't seem to matter much anymore; Ellis was far more focused on every human moment with Galen than with his inevitable transformation.

Galen's expression conveyed the same confusion. "Did… did we break it? I mean, a four-hour jump's got to mean someth—"

"I don't know. I don't care right now." He'd decided last night that it didn't matter anyway, and he wasn't going to get his hopes up now. Of course, now his brain was *back* on worrying about it, dammit. He shrugged it off. "Let's just take each minute as a gift right now." He grinned at the load of stuff Galen had succeeded in not dropping. "You've been busy."

Galen glanced at the terrarium and the pile of accessories. "Well, yeah, we knew we were going to need better accommodations for—" Blue focus returned to Ellis. "You don't care?"

"Not going to think about it right now." He eased closer to Galen, pulling slim hands over to rest on his waist. "If we make it to tomorrow morning at this time, I might consider celebrating. But I can't take getting excited now only to morph back in a minute or an hour or even six hours." And no point right now in explaining he truly didn't care anymore as long as he had this. He rested his forehead on Galen's shoulder.

Now a warm embrace enveloped him. "I understand. You said before you could feel winter pulling at you even when you were in human form. Do you still feel that?"

Good question. Ellis stood quiet for a moment, trying to listen to his body, his nerves, his… instinct. He couldn't tell what was instinct and what might simply be paranoia rearing its head. Galen's fingers in his hair didn't really help, nor the press of a tight form to his own. Confusion overcame any desire that might have stemmed from being naked in his lover's hold, though. After several moments, he sighed. "I don't know."

"Mm-kay." Galen pressed a kiss to his cheek and stepped back. "Well then, let's take your approach and stay in the moment. Ben called to tell me they got an invite to spend last night and today out at a friend's place on the Cape, so we'll have the house to ourselves until late tonight. I got breakfast along with the new frog digs, so let's eat and then set it all up. Just in case." A smirk of pure brat proportions lit Galen's face. "You might be warmer with some clothes on, though I won't complain if you decide to stay like that."

Ellis would have come back with equal wit if he could have gotten his heart to stop falling even further into thoughts of forever.

"**CLEARLY** the paperwork is not your niche." Ellis looked up from the laptop, watching the setting sun paint pure gold into Galen's hair through the bank of windows. "Have you seriously been doing this in seventy-five percent longhand for five years?" The pile of file folders had diminished two inches in the six hours they'd spent working.

Galen shrugged from his drafting table, where a detailed sketch of some new engine was taking shape. "I think better with pen and paper than a tablet. Usually Ben types the stuff up, but lately he's been bringing in new clients faster than we can keep up on the busywork. I think Joe simply voice-records everything and hopes the software can spell."

Ellis shook his head and reached for another file. "Incredible...."

"Hey, at least you can read my handwriting. Engineering school trains you to print in all caps. By the way, don't file Zimber or Moneer. Those are new clients sending me prototypes within the next two weeks. Just write the name on the end of the file folder and stick them in two of the rack slots over the desk." Galen glanced at the clock. "Wow, it's almost seven. That's... nineteen hours you've stayed human."

A nervous twitch, the one he'd managed to ignore while they worked, vibrated over his skin. "Don't jinx it. I wouldn't put it past Wayne to have set up some loophole to fuck with me for the rest of my life." He labeled the two files and set them in the rack.

"You really have a well-developed paranoid streak. But if he did we'll figure out how to get past it, even if I have to find an actual witchcraft correspondence course." Gentle hands eased over Ellis's shoulders. "Let's call it a day and relax. I'm starving. The guys won't be home until the wee hours of the morning at the earliest. More likely closer to noon. So why don't I go get us dinner? We can curl up together in the sauna after we eat, then maybe a movie on the big screen in the other room."

"Your folks planned for everything when they built this place." It sounded perfect, just as Galen's hands on his body felt perfect. Ellis sighed, leaning his head back to look up at his lover. "Yeah. Yeah, that works. Is there decent Indian food nearby?"

"Not just decent. Fucking fantastic Indian food." Galen leaned down and pressed a kiss to Ellis's cheek. "What's your preference and your spice level?"

Right now his preference was something other than food. He turned enough to kiss Galen properly without rupturing a disk, savoring the gasp he got as he slid his fingers up and around Galen's thigh. The moan from the back of Galen's throat made him stop, though, grinning up into a half glare. "Better stop. You have to go out in public for a little while." He still lifted the sweater hem and kissed the hollow of Galen's navel.

"God, I love you." Lean fingers tangled in his hair. "And the brat streak makes it all the more perfect. Tell me what you want for dinner and I'll be back before you get the files straightened up for the night."

Quiet settled over the space as Galen's phone conversation with the restaurant faded down the stairs and the front door closed with a soft thud. Ellis stacked the last of the reports on the desk and stood to stretch out his back. Being bipedal again still made his legs ache, a dull pressure whenever he moved, but no worse than after a rough gym workout. He intended to get dishes and silverware set up in the generous kitchenette at the bar in the game room; instead, he found himself detouring on the way, going through Galen's room to the upper terrace. It really was a nice little private space, secluded from the rest of the house by lush foliage in ornate pots that would likely come in soon or be emptied for the winter.

The light had faded from the windows, and a chill breeze hit his skin as he walked through the french doors. Dusk still backlit the skyline, but just above the city's glow the first bright stars glittered against a dark blue-gray. Ellis remembered the very first night he'd looked up at them from six feet closer to the ground, once the panic of being a frog had worn off. That had taken a week all by itself. But once he finally started for home, those stars had been the one thing he could count on to always be there, where they were supposed to be.

Now gazing up at them again, he tried to sort out his feelings, tried to remember what winter coming on had felt like. It was only a week ago he'd been drowning in that feeling, and now he could barely remember it.

Does that mean I'm cured? Or was it simply knowing he wouldn't be alone even if he did have to hibernate? The new terrarium they'd set up just this afternoon would provide a frog's version of a five-star hotel for the cold winter months and give him ample hiding space from Joe. That Galen would go to all this trouble for him left a warm spot radiating just under his ribcage.

And what if I am cured? Do I stay here? Do I go home?

Going home, at least to let his parents know he was all right, was a given. Even if the thought of it currently left him a bit weary. And at the moment he had no idea how to explain where he'd been for a year that wouldn't land him in a padded room. But still….

Doubtless his father would immediately resurrect all the plans for Ellis to step in and manage the portfolio and the various investments. None of which had ever interested Ellis in the least. While he hadn't exactly figured out *what* he wanted to do with his life, he did know he wanted to *do* something, not simply earn on his investments while he puttered around with golf or sailing or whatever. His mother had her hobbies, the horses, and her various clubs. He just couldn't think of anything he did as recreation that he'd want to do *all* the time.

Watching Galen and his brothers plow into helping small start-ups, get their hands into something that would lead to something better, fascinated him. And while he might not be a financier, a marketer, or an engineer, he'd always been good at organizing. His father seemed to consider administrative skills useful but generally beneath him, so Ellis knew it was likely his own interest would be met with some mild disdain. He'd have to figure out how to reach an understanding on that. And his father would be impressed that the Townsend brothers made it possible for new entrepreneurs to get a fair start, so there was that. Being a part of it could satisfy them both.

And God knew Galen at least could use an administrative assistant. Ellis would just have to find a way to come back with minimal hard feelings at the change to Dad's plans.

The lights came on across the backyard area, enough to navigate without disturbing the serenity of the evening. Ellis glanced down at the gazebo, the pond nearby with the Adirondack lounge not yet put away for the season. What a different result had stemmed from his expectations! The pond had seemed like a safe haven for the winter even if it didn't net him his princess; instead, he'd found love and hopefully the cure to the spell.

"You're thinking awfully loud."

Ellis turned at the sound of Galen's voice. "Just watching the stars. Spent a lot of summer nights over the past year doing that. Always took them for granted before they became the only steady thing in my life."

"That's one of my favorite things to do. I track the meteor showers every year. We get a little light pollution from Boston in the distance and the train station here, but not too bad. The woods Dad left around the perimeter filter a lot of it. I turn off the grounds lighting and it's nearly dark skies." Galen wrapped his arms around Ellis's waist from behind. "We'll make a date of it."

A simple, comfortable life. A purpose that helped more than just himself. If anything good had come from Wayne's Warlockian Wonderfuck, Ellis considered this more than worth the mess.

GALEN woke to a beautiful sight. Ellis, lying on his stomach, arms curled around a pillow, pale blond strands in disarray over his face, blanket and sheet pushed down around lean hips, the teasing glimpse of a tight ass peeking from the edge. They'd now passed twenty-four hours without a morph and were approaching thirty-six. Galen allowed himself to level up on hope that they'd broken the spell.

Working together yesterday had been incredible. Days and days like that, months, years… it all flowed so perfectly in his mind.

But how long did they have before Ellis went home to whatever waited for him, was expected of him? How long before the dream became only that?

Ellis stirred, turning onto his back, one arm across his eyes. The blanket shifted farther down, wrapping tighter, just barely covering intimate flesh. God, he looked like a model for a magazine. Galen reached over and teased one fingertip lightly into the edge of pale curls, grinning at the moan he got in response. Time for a little payback for Monday night's sensual torture over dinner. With as glorious an ending.

Barely-there strokes, long and lingering, tracing the subtle contours of muscle on Ellis's abdomen and chest, circling his nipples, never going lower than the edge of the blanket. Galen watched arousal rise and strain against the secured fabric. Ellis moaned again, hands reaching to press Galen's touch harder.

"Uh-uh." Galen eased up, moving to straddle Ellis and secure the blanket further, taking Ellis's hands and raising them over his head to slip through the brass rails of the headboard. The necktie he hadn't put away from last week's dinner out hung neatly between the headboard and the support post and made an excellent soft restraint. Target secured, Galen returned to the slow exploration of his lover.

Ellis opened sleepy green eyes, a smile curving one corner of his mouth. "Not what I expected from you, but not complaining. Morning, gorgeous. You planning on moving that blanket anytime soon?

"Nope." Galen slid up to straddle Ellis's chest, moving his touch up onto Ellis's neck, collarbone, shoulders. The shiver as he stroked Ellis's lips and cheeks fired his blood with a soft passion. How the hell was he supposed to let this go?

Ellis's smile gained a touch of imp as he gazed down over Galen's naked body. "Planning on making me wake you up further?"

"Wasn't thinking of that, but…." Galen considered what sort of a mood he was in. "Long as you don't get too hot and heavy on me. I'm in Lazy Sunday mode right now."

"Lazy Sunday is bondage? Can't wait to see you on a tear." Ellis wiggled until he could just kiss Galen's thigh. "Come up a little farther then, before I tear a tendon trying to get to you."

God, that warm mouth around him! Galen gripped the headboard rail, letting Ellis set the rhythm and depth, and let his mind blank to everything but sensation.

A soft chuckle brought him from his reverie, and he eased out of his lover's mouth. "What?"

"You are mellow this morning." Ellis licked a drop from the corner of his lips. "I like it. We stay at this pace, we could last half the day."

God, the thought of every Sunday spent loving each other slowly…. Galen shifted down so he straddled Ellis's knees, then peeled the blanket back just far enough to expose rigid arousal but not enough so Ellis could move his legs. The light in Ellis's eyes warmed him in the cool morning air.

"My turn." Galen leaned over and blew a soft breath over Ellis's tip, getting a deep groan for his effort. Lightly, he kissed the tip, then slid his tongue along the groove and down around the head of his lover's shaft, taking as long as he could comfortably manage.

"Fuck yeah…." Another more vehement curse followed when Galen detoured up to circle Ellis's navel, letting Ellis's shaft trail down Galen's chest in the process. Galen repeated the entire loop twice more, each round hitching Ellis's breath further. Slim fingers wrapped around the headboard spindles; narrow hips thrust upward in plea. "Galen…."

"Mmm…." He drew Ellis's erection into his mouth for a single long moment, sucking softly as he drew back. He waited until Ellis whimpered and shifted upward again before repeating the same single stroke.

Ellis panted, long deep breaths expanding his chest. "Shit, that's good." It took two more breaths before he spoke again. "Shit, I gotta think about those goddamn snakes in the pond grasses just to keep from spoiling your slow-route plans." He grinned at the brow Galen raised. "Trust me, being hunted by an adult one kills all the double-entendres pretty much forever."

"You ready for more?"

"God yeah."

Galen stretched out over his lover, bodies touching from toes to chest, arousals shifting against each other. He thrust in slow short movements as he savored Ellis's mouth. Lovemaking had never been like this before, and if he had to let it go, he'd damn well make sure it was unlikely to be as good ever again.

"Galen, untie me. Please. I want to touch you back. I want to hold you." Ellis trailed a kiss over to Galen's ear. "Please, babe. God, I want you so much."

"Mm-kay." He loosened the tie but stayed where he was, allowing Ellis to touch but not move. "But you stay put." He moved off the blanket pinning Ellis's legs, finally pushing it toward the foot of the bed. He took Ellis's mouth with slow thoroughness, then settled on his side with his head propped up on one arm. The other hand stroked flat planes over Ellis's abdomen, hard enough to comfort without tickling. He moved Ellis's hand away when his lover tried to do more than just cuddle. "Uh-uh. My lead. Let's take a break." The muffled curse under Ellis's breath made Galen grin. "See what you have to look forward to? Am I still worth it?"

Pale green eyes lanced him to the heart. "Yes. Do you even have to ask that? I love you, Galen. Go figure, huh? Falling in love in a week's time… I always thought that was just romance-novel stuff." Ellis shifted his hips closer. "I don't quite know how I'm going to work it, but I want to stay here. With you. For the rest of our lives."

Could it be? Could they really have that? Galen wasn't sure he dared hope that far.

Ellis's gaze searched over him. "You…. Last night you said you felt the same. You still… I mean…."

"Shh." Galen kissed away the soft stutter. "Yes. I do. I love you too, Ellis. And I want that. Being together. I'm just having a hard time letting it become a real possibility in my heart, that's all. Because I don't know what I'll do if we can't work things out."

"Hell, you kissed a fucking frog on nothing more than boredom and half a guilt trip." Gentle fingers trailed comfort over his cheek. "I took the insane leap of tracking you down for a second one. We can do fucking anything together." Ellis reached between them to fondle gently. "Let me hold you. Touch you while you take me. We both need to know we can do this."

Galen nodded, shrugging away a tear that had escaped his control. He captured Ellis's mouth again; the morning air had chilled Ellis's hands, making Galen shiver as nimble fingers caressed him. But rather than distracting, it only warmed Galen's heart more.

Kisses turned deep, caresses more insistent. Ellis's pleas in Galen's ear as they rutted against each other added fuel to the fire. A quick foray into the nightstand drawer for lube and a condom, and Galen pinned Ellis's legs again, spread this time so he could reach down to massage Ellis's balls and then slip one finger inside his lover.

"Ngggh… oh fuck, yeah…." Ellis thrust hard toward Galen's touch, hips in time with the rhythm of Galen sucking one hard nipple. "Please… oh shit, please,…."

A moment's pause to prepare himself and Galen eased into glorious heat, tight muscles closing around him, capturing him. A harder thrust produced a high sob from Ellis, pale hair thrown back across the pillow, paler skin glowing in the sunrise light.

"Oh God, Galen, I'm gonna—"

Galen straightened and caught the base of Ellis's shaft in a tight grip. "No, you're not. Not yet. You're going to come with me, and I'm not quite there yet." He drew most of the way out and thrust hard again. Then again. And again.

"ShitshitfuckshitfuckGod— Shit!" Ellis turned his face against the pillow and screamed, still meeting Galen's thrusts. "Oh God, faster. Faster, Galen, please…." Another muffled scream followed.

Wow, he's beautiful like this. Ellis was stunning anyway, but right now Galen still had enough coherency—in fact, the sight *kept* him coherent long past his expectations—to truly enjoy the sight of his lover coming apart.

Only when he'd reduced Ellis to a simple whispered litany of "God" and "please" did Galen loosen his grip and allow his own passion to spike. The world went white and a warm wet splash coated his stomach. If Ellis screamed again, it never made it past the roaring in Galen's ears.

By the time he could see again, Galen had collapsed on top of Ellis, who still panted like a freight train, long deep gulps of air whooshing out through his teeth.

"Oh. My. Fucking. God. That was a goddamned fucking work of art. Do they give out Oscars for sex? I can have a lifetime of this?"

Galen felt a laugh bubble up and let it loose. "Always nice to get good reviews." He managed enough energy to move to Ellis's side. "I'd hug you right now, but I'm scared we'd end up glued together."

"Here." Ellis sat up to grab the end of the sheet and settle it between them. He lay back down and pulled Galen close. "Now we can cuddle until we can move."

Simply lying in bed together felt as good as the sex. Galen pressed a kiss to Ellis's cheek. "You know, we really don't have that much to do today. The guys seem to like 'Roland' well enough. They wouldn't be too surprised to see you here again. We could always—"

He was interrupted by the chime of the front doorbell. Galen glanced at the clock. Who on earth could be ringing at 9:00 a.m. on a Sunday morning? Everyone knew the Townsend boys played hard and late on the weekends. Did his brothers forget to lock the gate? Joe maybe, but Ben? Or had he forgotten it himself when he came home with dinner? He'd been thinking more about Ellis than—

"Galen!" Ben's voice carried up the stairs. "There's a guy here to see you. Says he needs to talk to you urgently."

Shit. Someone's home? Had Ben heard them? God, he'd never hear the end of the Switzerland Rule without admitting he had a… well, *semi*-permanent at this point… lover in the house. *I am so not ready to come up with that whole story yet.* Galen reached for his robe as he staggered to the door and cracked it open. "He give a name?" He was not getting properly out of bed for some salesman.

A pause. "Says his name is Neville Faraday. He's from New Hampshire?"

Ellis shot up in the bed, eyes wide and face ashen. "Neville Faraday? That's my father."

Chapter Ten

GALEN sucked in a breath as he approached the parlor. Having to meet Ellis's father with no warning, a sixty-second rinse, last night's clothes tossed on, no coffee, no breakfast—and no Ellis beside him—was about as far from perfect as it could be. But of course Ellis *couldn't* be at his side just yet. Little hard to explain where the hell you'd been for the last year—being a frog, not so credible if you hadn't actually seen or been it—and then show up with a boyfriend. Hell, right now Galen's own brothers didn't know Ellis was staying here. Only that there was a "Roland" who'd been over a couple times.

The elder Faraday rose from one of the leather wing chairs, with some assistance from an elegant brass-topped cane, to greet Galen. A fair resemblance, the same long, lean build, the same softness to the eyes. But instead of Ellis's impish twinkle, Neville Faraday's gaze held exhaustion and grief. Broad shoulders might have stooped from age, but Galen suspected the burden of searching for a missing son had probably bowed them further.

"Mr. Townsend." A resonant voice accustomed to command, though rough with either desperation or hope. "I understand you may have some information regarding my missing son."

Galen blinked and noted Ben's eyebrows climbing, but accepted the handshake. Clearly Dena hadn't let the chance meeting at the restaurant go, in spite of Ellis's little subterfuge. "Um... I'm sorry, how—"

"How did I find you? The young lady who exercises my wife's horses related a recent incident of seeing a man who could be my son's twin having dinner at a restaurant while she was visiting her cousin here. She took a covert photo after she left speaking with you. Armed with that, it didn't take her long to find someone in the area who knew your name. The rest took very little investigation."

"I see." Galen gestured Ellis's father back to the wing chair and took the matching one for himself. Okay, so how the hell did he handle this? What if Mr. Faraday asked him flat-out if his dinner companion was Ellis? Or flat-out if he'd seen Ellis? What if—

"I was wondering if you could arrange for me to meet your dinner companion. Obviously I'd like to see for myself, and pose a question or two to the young man." The genteel mask faltered a moment, and long fingers curled into broad palms. "My son has been missing for a year, Mr. Townsend. No trace, no trail beyond the last place he was seen with a companion.

The police have theorized everything from abduction to suicide to… well, everything in between. You can understand how the report I received…."

Bet they didn't theorize on what really happened, since the news article said they figured Wayne's interview was fantasy. Galen kept his smirk to himself. "Yes, sir. I do understand." He felt for the man. Ellis might have gone on about a lack of interest in the business relationship, but the close familial connection was as clear in Mr. Faraday's voice and body language as it was in Ellis's. "I think my friend would be willing to sit down with you. Are you free this evening? I can arrange for you to meet here." Explaining all this to his brothers would be a chore, but here was probably the most comfortable solution for everyone involved. And it had been thirty-six hours now since Ellis was last a frog.

"Oh yes, I'm free. Indeed I am." The light in Mr. Faraday's eyes…. Yep, here was going to be the best choice all around. The older man stood as Galen did, clasping Galen's hand again, covering their clasped hands with his free one. "Seven, perhaps? Eight? Whatever is best for you."

"Let's say seven." No point dragging out the man's agony. And seven would still give Ellis plenty of time for whatever not-frog explanation he planned on. And if Ellis turned into a frog again between now and seven… well, they'd figure something out that wouldn't devastate the man further. Galen retrieved his hand and gestured them back toward the foyer. He paused to shake Mr. Faraday's hand again. "I hope you find what you're looking for, sir."

"Oh, so do I, young man. So do I." Ellis's father gathered up a fine overcoat and a felt fedora, then grasped Galen's shoulder. He looked easily five years younger than when he'd walked in. "Thank you, thank you so very much. Good day to you, good day. I'll see you tonight."

Galen stood at the open doorway for a few seconds more, watching the solitary figure walk back to a chauffeured Lexus. He'd have been happier if he could have found something to dislike, but Neville Faraday seemed a genuinely good man devastated over the loss of his son. And that made it all the more difficult.

"Is this about that Rollie guy?" Ben's voice at his shoulder dragged him from the ache in his heart. "Faraday…. Faraday…. Hey, wasn't that the name on that wet and muddy designer suit I found out by the gazebo? What the hell is going on, Galen?"

"You'd never believe me if I told you." Dead serious, that. "Or you'd have me committed."

"Try me."

"Uhh…." It sounded insane rehearsed in his head, especially since Ellis wouldn't hopefully—be morphing back into a frog ever again. So no proof, nothing but a completely batshit-sounding story. He chickened out. "I'm not sure of all the details myself." Truth, for the most part at least.

"Wuss."

Damn straight.

"You need to be nosier, little brother." Ben pushed the door closed. "By the way, did you have company last night? Sounded this morning like you might have."

Shit. Galen felt the blush flood downward from his ears. "Yeah, sorry, I know, the house is Switzerland. We got talking really late."

His brother nodded. "You know, if it's serious, we can probably start to ease up on the Switzerland rule. You've seemed happier, content, over the past week or so."

"I was. I mean, I am." If only it weren't all about to take a sharp curve sideways. "We'll see."

"M-kay. Anyway, Joe's making pancakes if you're interested. And if your friend's interested. They should be hot off the griddle about now. Which is why he wasn't eavesdropping at the kitchen doorway just now and why you may have to summarize all this again." A comforting hand clapped his shoulder. "Go get your houseguest. Come eat something. Take the ribbing from Joe like a trouper. Figure out the rest later."

Yeah, that sounded pretty good.

"SO what are you going to tell him?" Galen shifted his ass further into his work chair while Ellis paced the length of Galen's office.

He could barely form a thought, with his heart racing and his brain fucking mush. The decent breakfast sat like a rock in his stomach, despite the fact he'd gotten along quite well with Galen's brothers in the first brief meeting. "I don't know. Hey, Dad, you remember that guy Wayne I was seeing a year back? The one who spouted all that bullshit to the police about what happened? Yeah, well, it's all true. He got weird on me and I decided to duck out early on the long weekend, and then he turned me into a frog. For real. He's a warlock, y'see, the whole black magick schtick, and he's really good." Dear God, they'd have him in a padded room before the echo died on that bit of *Twilight Zone*. "I've spent the last year hopping home, with a short train ride here and there before I had to get off and find water or someone freaked out, and I only got as far as mid-Massachusetts because, you know, *frog*, and winter came and I had to hibernate for four months…. Yeah, that'll go over just fucking great." He resumed his pacing, hoping at some point he'd stumble upon a better story.

"Well, the part about Wayne being at the heart of your disappearance would work. Far as I'm concerned, he might as well have kidnapped you." Galen reached for a pencil off his drafting board and began drumming it absently on his thigh. "They'll never prove anything, of course, but you might get past your dad with that."

Was it really that simple? Or would Neville Faraday use his considerable influence to have Wayne arrested, regardless of what could or couldn't be proved?

"Can't say you just decided to take a year and find yourself. They'd wonder why you hadn't said anything about it to them or contacted them, right?"

No, that wouldn't work. While Ellis's parents weren't into spontaneous hugs and kisses, they'd always been supportive and encouraging. Logical, sensible. Loving in their own ways.

His father had grown up resisting every attempt to codify him by wealth or social status, and he'd raised Ellis that way as well. He lived by the credo that wealth was a responsibility rather than a privilege, and that one only truly prospered by making sure the rest of society did as well. But he kept a treasured inner circle: his family, close friends, and business contacts, checking in often to make sure they were all right. So while seeking a purpose in life would be readily accepted, zero contact would not.

His mother had read books to him as a child and arranged for the resources to follow any interest he had, but she wasn't really the cookie-baking or macaroni-necklace sort. A part-time nanny had filled in most of the hands-on blanks. But he knew she'd been every bit as frantic as his father over his disappearance. And she wouldn't have come on this little fishing expedition; if it turned out to be a hoax, it would be too much for her. Ellis suspected she was out in the stables seeking comfort from her horses and would stay there most of the afternoon and late into the evening, waiting for his father to call.

They'd been his first thought for support when his world went to hell. Even in those first moments of panic, when he'd realized the touchscreen of his phone wouldn't take frog fingers, he'd careened around Wayne's flat and out the window to the fire escape and then the street, dodging feet and bicycles, toward the first train station that would take him north. Home. Even after he'd had to pause and take stock out of sheer necessity—and breath, and water—his foremost thought had been to get to them, though he'd had no clue what he'd have done when he got there. He might have spent the rest of his life watching them from a distance, from the lake. But he would be *near* them.

Ellis realized his thoughts had wandered off on a tangent and shook himself back to the present. What the hell was he going to come up with?

He sighed, noting that Galen had simply waited for him to finish his mental wanderings without any impatience and loving him all the more for it. "I guess it's Wayne for the win. So how do I make this sound credible without landing Wayne in the electric

chair? I mean, he didn't actually hurt me, just...
made me a frog."

Galen got up and tossed the pencil to Ellis. "Well,
let's sketch it out on the board here." He switched to a
dry-erase marker, flipping it over with a flourish before
taking the cap off. "We'll have it polished up in no
time."

THE clock in the parlor had clearly slowed time down
on purpose just to make him squirm. The beveled glass
panes of the front door, visible between the wide,
columned archways, seemed to be staring at him,
glaring at him, boring a hole right between his eyes.
Ellis twitched and got up from the wing chair for the
fourth time in as many minutes, circled it once, and sat
down again. If he paced any more, he'd pull a quad.

"Here." Galen handed him a lowball glass half
filled with... bourbon, from the smell. "Maybe that'll
calm you down."

"Nothing's going to calm me down." He drained
the drink without tasting it; the burn barely registered
in his throat. "What time is it?" No matter he'd been
looking at the clock before the booze showed up.

"It's 6:53. You said your dad is super-punctual."
Galen retrieved the empty glass and set it on the bar.
"For all we know, he's sitting in his Lexus in the
driveway staring at his watch. You need to breathe,
Ellis. It'll be okay."

Okay. Okay. What was "okay"? What combination
of events would end in "okay"? If there was a definition
of "okay" for this situation, he had no fucking idea
what it might be. He rubbed his hands on his thighs,
hoping there wouldn't be dark stains on the jeans

from the amount of cold sweat coming off his palms. One knee decided to start bouncing, setting his entire skeleton vibrating in a not-fun way. Nothing felt comfortable. His skin itched. From the inside. And he was reasonably sure he could live on earthworms again if he had to, because his stomach was so tightly clenched it probably couldn't hold more than two of the little fuckers at a time.

The fact that the doorbell rang *exactly* between the third and fourth chimes of 7:00 p.m. weirded him out even further. Ellis stood and tried to get a grip on his shaking hands before the tremors spread to the rest of his body. He ducked into a corner of the parlor where a large potted fern hid him from immediate view. *Maybe this was a bad idea. Maybe he's going to hate me. Maybe I should have just stayed in that goddamn pond and not said a word.* And maybe his chest would implode at any second. It sure felt like it might.

Galen had gone to answer the door, and now voices filtered to Ellis's hearing.

"Mr. Townsend, so good to see you again. Were you able to get in touch with your friend?" His dad sounded… eager. Hopeful. A bit desperate. Ellis tried to not let guilt creep into his soul along with everything else. It really wasn't his fault he'd been a frog. God, breathing hurt.

"Yes, sir, he's waiting in the parlor. Let me take your coat and hat." Okay, so a few brain cells worked on something other than panic. He hadn't had a chance to realize how mannered Galen really was. *Dad'll like that. Classy and all.*

Then the dragging time caught up in one painful breath and he was facing a man he hadn't seen in a year. Calm, kind blue eyes gone very wide. A gasp and the stiffening of a lean frame, a broad hand clenching tightly over the deer's head topper of his cane. His father's face had gained some deep lines; Ellis did feel a pinch of guilt at that, and gripped the edge of the table holding the fern. But his dad. A man Ellis had thought he might never see again, or only from a distance as he lived out the rest of his life as a frog. And it still wouldn't have been more than a few years even if he managed to not get eaten or run over. A new weight shook his knees; his heart contracted further from more than the dash of guilt.

His father didn't seem to be much steadier, reaching out his free hand to grasp Galen's shoulder. "Dear God. Dena said there was a resemblance, but my God...." Glancing over at Galen, as if to confirm, his dad took a single step farther into the room, astonished and not a little wary. Understandable, since he was clearly hoping against hope. It showed in the shine over his eyes. "Young man, are you... could you possibly be...."

The utter exhaustion on that dear face was the last blow to any real control. Everything rushed in on him, and Ellis couldn't stay composed. His posture went to hell as the feeling of his chest caving in tightened every muscle and his vision tunneled. Tears filled his eyes and clogged his throat, and he managed a shaky nod as the tremors won. His voice could easily have been the croak of a real frog. "Yeah, Dad, it's me."

"Oh my God. Ellis." If there was a lecture coming, it wasn't cued up yet. A quick huff of laughter, the sudden flash of a bright white smile, and his dad crossed the space between them in three long strides to gather Ellis up in a hug tight enough to strangle. Matching tears warmed Ellis's shirt collar for several moments as they clung to each other. His remaining composure shattered, and he sobbed into his father's shoulder, barely able to remain standing. He could feel his father shaking even as solid arms held him up.

By the time they pulled apart, Galen had set two new drinks and a box of tissues on the end table between the wing chairs. He smiled at Ellis. "Would you like to talk alone?"

"No, I want you here. Please." Ellis wiped the worst of the tears from his eyes so he could see, and gestured his father to a chair. "Dad, I—"

"Where have you been? What happened to you?" His father perched on the edge of the chair seat but kept a hand on Ellis's arm across the end table. "The last we heard from you was when you went to New York for a long weekend. What happened?"

Cover story time. Ellis sucked in a breath, glanced over at Galen—who had settled on one of the barstools—for a dose of support, and tried out the first part of it. "I, um… well, do you remember that guy Wayne I met a couple summers back?"

"Yes. Strange young man, though I could never put my finger on exactly why he seemed that way." His dad let go of Ellis's arm just long enough for a generous sip of his drink. "You're saying you were with him? But you never called, never—"

Ellis held up a hand. "I wasn't actually… *with him*. Not the way you think." Shit, this was going to be harder than he thought. "He… well, he sort of wanted to keep me around and wasn't taking no for an answer. He… sort of took control of my life." True, if it came down to technical details.

"He abducted… *held you*? Prisoner?" Ellis didn't often see his father's temper, but on the occasions when it did surface, it always built and crashed like a thunderstorm coming in off the sea. Now it roiled to hurricane level at the speed of a lightning flash and darkened his father's whole countenance. "What did he do to you? Did he hurt you?"

"No, Dad, no. I'm fine." Ellis leaned forward to lay his hand over his father's. "I wasn't... it wasn't.... He smashed my phone and wouldn't let me leave. Locked me in a bedroom whenever he went out. That was basically it. He didn't hurt me. He didn't try... anything against my will. He just didn't want me to go."

Generous graying eyebrows drew together. "He should still be held to account. You didn't try to fight him? To escape? For a year?"

Dammit, here was where it would get messy. Ellis focused on the fancy parlor rug and tried to remember what he and Galen had discussed earlier. Soft footsteps and the warm hand now resting on his shoulder were welcome, but it really didn't help him think.

"He— I was confused for some of it. A lot of it. It was worse when he went out. Couldn't really focus properly." True, if you took into account the initial panic attack and then the weeks of trying to figure out what exactly one did as a frog.

"So he drugged you." His father sat back, a deep, icy anger darkening his eyes to almost charcoal. "I want you thoroughly checked out by our physician, and a psychiatrist, when we get home. Then I'm going to get Moira Coughlin to tell me exactly what our legal options are."

A quick glance up at Galen revealed the same pang Ellis had felt clench at his heart. *I don't want to go home. I want to stay here with you.* But of course they both knew that wasn't possible, not now at least.

The tap of his father's cane on the floor brought his attention back around. "How did you finally escape? And how did you end up here when you could have simply found a telephone? Or a train?"

This part they'd managed rather well, Ellis thought. "Wayne had a thing Friday before last, and apparently thought after a year I was cowed or confused enough to stay put with him. It was the first time he'd ever brought me along, the first chance I had to get away. He was in this neighborhood, so I just headed for the first house I could. I was pretty out of it, I guess." More or less credible.

Galen smiled. "Caught me by surprise, I'll admit. It's really only in the last few days he's felt completely himself. He wanted to make sure he was okay before he called you." That was the absolute truth.

His father stared at Ellis for a long moment. Ellis tried to not twitch; it really was as close to the truth as they could get without going into the completely batshit version.

"And going to dinner, where Dena saw you? The subterfuge? Why didn't you simply tell her who you were?"

Dammit, every detail…. "I…. Like Galen said, I wanted to be sure I was fully recovered before I contacted anyone. I wasn't expecting to see anyone I knew. I guess I panicked again or something. I collapsed again when we got h— back here. Too much too fast, I guess." Ellis served that up with a shrug. "I certainly never expected her to tell you. I'd have thought she'd have more sense than to drum up false hope by saying she saw a dead ringer for me. I was planning to call you, or arrange a trip home, tomorrow." Okay, it might have been later in the week, but he'd known he'd have to make contact very soon.

Now the sharp gaze turned to Galen. "And you, young man. You didn't immediately call the police because—"

Oh God. Ellis leaned forward in his own chair. "I asked him not to, Dad. I really was a wreck, and I just wanted to... you know, stop and regroup for a sec before I had to explain it to someone. I wasn't making much sense when I first got here. I could barely tell Galen, let alone the cops. And like I said, Wayne didn't hurt me. I don't want to have to deal with him again with the cops." Please, please, *please* let that be enough.

After a moment, which dragged by every bit as slowly as the minutes before this reunion, his father nodded. "I understand. You were very fortunate to have found a kind benefactor." Now the gaze at Galen softened into a smile.

Thank you, Universe, and that list of deities from the Pig Incident.

"Well. You're back now, and you seem to be none the worse for wear. You're still going to the doctor, and we're still going to talk to the lawyer." His father stood, straightening his suit jacket and tie. Emotional moments never stuck around very long, not on the surface anyway. "Why don't you gather up whatever you might have acquired in your stay here and we'll head back to the hotel and call your mother. We'll leave for home in the morning."

Ellis felt the blood rush from his head. Just like that? No real goodbye, no chance to assure Galen he'd be back sometime, somehow?

Galen's color didn't look much better, but he offered a smile as he rested his arms on the back of the armchair Ellis sat in. "You know, sir, you've both been through a bit of an emotional wringer. It's nearly eight now. If you'd like some time to… well, process everything, Ellis could stay here one more night and you could pick him up in the morning. Save you rearranging your hotel space."

Oh please, Dad, please. It's logical and kind and you like all that, so please, I am so begging…. Ellis managed to get to his feet without letting on he was close to another panic attack.

"Thank you, Mr. Townsend. Galen, was it? That's very kind of you." Ellis knew full well his father's anger hadn't cooled, and he would welcome some time alone even though there might be the tiniest sliver of anxiety that Ellis would vanish again, but the anger wasn't directed at Galen and the genteel smile was back. "In fact, I thank you wholeheartedly for caring for my son, even though he showed up as a stranger on your doorstep. Many wouldn't."

You have no idea, Dad. Try it as an amphibian.

Galen shook the proffered hand. "It was no trouble at all, sir. I found a good, good friend in the process."

His dad glanced between them, and Ellis couldn't tell what thoughts went on behind those light blue eyes. "I'm so glad you did. I—" Then Ellis was pulled into another abrupt embrace, no less exuberant than the initial shocked greeting. "Welcome home, son. Welcome home. I'll— I'll see you bright and early. We've got a drive. Oh, your mother will be so very happy to see you!" He pulled out his phone. "We need to call her right now. She'll want to know I've found you and to at least hear your voice for a moment. I suspect she'll be crying too much to ask more than if you're all right. We can tell her all the rest when we get home."

"Yeah." Whatever else he might have said stuck in his throat as he sank back into the chair. The flood of emotion might have gotten away from him if it wasn't for Galen's fingers drifting discreetly over the back of his head.

As predicted, his mother's reaction had been much the same as his father's, filled with tears and joy, but without all the questions. Those would come later, Ellis knew, but for now he simply basked in hearing her again.

After a few moments his father retrieved the phone. "Yes, darling, we're heading home first thing in the morning. No, I don't think we're ready for that just yet, but I know you'll call them all anyway to let them know. Just family for now. I think Ellis has been through enough at the moment. It'll wait. We'll see you tomorrow. Good night." His father pocketed the phone.

Ellis had barely regained his composure again when his dad drew him up into another hug. "I'm still convincing myself you're really here. You'll have to put up with it, I fear, for the next several weeks. My son, my son." A watery chuckle ruffled Ellis's hair before his father pulled back. "Oh, I'm a complete wreck, aren't I? But then I have excellent reason. I'll go now, before I break down completely and embarrass you. Bright and early, my boy, bright and early...."

The litany continued from the parlor to the door and as his father collected his coat and quite nearly skipped out to his waiting car. The smile as he waved before getting in could have powered the entire state.

Ellis embraced Galen from behind as the car pulled away and smothered a grin against his lover's hair. "I expected him to be glad to see me, but…."

"You're lucky. You still have him here, warts and all. I miss my dad." Galen turned and slipped an arm around Ellis's waist. "You okay? That explanation seemed to work all right."

"I'll just have to convince him to not bother trying to sue Wayne. That smug little bastard knows there's no proof anyway." He lowered his voice to a whisper in case Galen's brothers were listening in from somewhere. "But I'm going to find another warlock or witch or something and see if there's some sort of a shield against future frog spells. Someone with a little more experience than you at the moment." Ellis took Galen's laugh as an excuse to capture a welcome mouth. He'd take every minute they had left until tomorrow morning to make sure Galen knew just how very much he was loved.

GALEN'S brothers, fortunately, had chosen to eavesdrop from the kitchen, so there were only a few questions about why the hell Galen hadn't said anything about the charity case hiding in the upstairs guest suite. And thank God neither of them thought to ask why Molly hadn't noticed, though Galen had added to the plan a bit about not knowing how she'd react so they'd hidden him in the sauna while she was cleaning. Probably the diciest part of the story, but they didn't have to use it. The cover story of post-drugged and panicked worked fairly well for the rest. The growing friendship and potential relationship for little brother took care of any lingering doubts or suspicions.

They'd also been perceptive enough—Ben, at least—to declare a Marvel marathon and hole up in the cinema room. Now the house was silent again, except for Galen's breathing over a Corona bottle at the kitchen island. Ellis didn't have to see his lover's face, half-shielded by the hand supporting Galen's head, to know long eyelashes would be starred with tears, but he could see the tension in Galen's jaw, set against a flood of emotion.

His own limbs felt heavy as he held up the breakfast bar tucked against the back stairs, hands shoved in his pockets, even a faint smile taking some effort at the moment. Less than four feet separated them, but for all the connection he could feel from Galen right now, it could have been a mile.

Dammit, I don't want to spend our last night together like this. Ellis pulled in a breath and nodded to himself for enough of an ass kick to cross those four feet and move the other island stool out of the way so he could lean back against the granite counter, close enough his thigh brushed Galen's. "You feel like takeout?"

"Not really."

Ellis internalized a sigh. "Delivery?"

"Not really." Galen's shoulders slumped, and the weight of his head seemed to be too much for his arm. Ellis really hadn't expected the emotional role reversal; until now Galen had been the optimist. Now it seemed to take all his friend had to form that two-word sentence.

Okay, easy questions weren't doing the trick, so Ellis opted for a little soft snark. "I am a year out of practice with a stove, dude. And I'm hardly Alton Brown, even on my best day."

"I'm not really hungry." Galen scratched at the beer label with his fingernail, but Ellis would lay money he didn't actually see it right now.

"Me either. But we didn't eat before Dad showed up. I think I'd have tossed it up five minutes later if I had." Ellis nudged Galen's leg and reached over to take Galen's hand. "I figure we might need at least a little fuel for the rest of the evening, though."

The hard swallow and the shine in Galen's eyes as he looked up nearly demolished Ellis's resolve to not spend their last night together for a while sobbing their fucking guts out.

"I don't want you to go." Galen's voice broke, and he swallowed again. Ellis's throat hurt just watching. "I know you have to. I just don't want…."

"Absolutely feel you, man. But you're not losing me. This is nothing more than a little logistical detour." Ellis kept hold of Galen's hand and ran his free fingertips over the short soft buzz at the back of Galen's neck. "We'll make sure I give you at least the landline number before I leave. God knows when I'll have a new phone or what I'll have to do to get one, being a missing person or whatever. My credit is probably hosed. And I'll get your email and phone. It'll be okay. Let's just be together tonight without the impending doom hovering over us." He bent to slide his lips over Galen's and didn't let up until he felt his lover relax completely.

Galen kept Ellis in his embrace even after they separated, lips settled on Ellis's collarbone for several more minutes. Just resting. Dear lord, it felt every bit as amazing to Ellis as full-on sex. Simply being there for each other. He pressed kisses into Galen's hair and waited for the worst to pass.

Finally, a deep sigh tickled through Ellis's shirt. "We can eat out of the freezer. Ben gets on a cooking kick once in a while, after an especially argumentative client encounter. He makes enough food for half the city before he calms down."

"I remember the empanadas discussion. Sounds like a plan." Ellis pressed one more kiss into Galen's hair and then headed for the fridge. It felt normal, making a simple meal together. Familiar. *Right.* That alone should tell him something, seeing as they still barely knew each other even after a week of talking. They hadn't really gone much deeper than music, movies, a brief recount of Galen's parents' death, and the systematic upending of Ellis's life. He had a fair idea of Galen's core habits and quirks. But still basic surface stuff. Ellis vowed to do a little more digging before he left, without making a production of it.

Might as well start while he warmed up... hmm, garlic chicken, lasagna, something labeled *OTTOMH.* Ellis couldn't help but laugh. "Ottomh? What's that, dare I ask?"

Galen had returned to his self-hypnosis via beer bottle. "'Off the top of my head.' Sort of a stew, I guess. I think it results from what's left over when Ben's done with the real recipes. It's usually decent, though it's different every time." He still hadn't managed enough energy to get his voice out of monotone.

"Think I'll pass for tonight." Ellis grabbed two servings of the garlic chicken and instigated another mental ass kick as he closed the freezer door. "So, let's see... neatnik, right? At least aside from your office files."

"Huh?" Galen looked up at least.

"I saw breakfast last Wednesday. And the place is too tidy for just your housekeeper once a week. Betting you guys are more or less self-cleaning." Ellis grinned at the expression he got. "Dude, we've been together for a week-plus. I love you, but I don't know shit about you. Other than you're smart, a smartass, kind to amphibians, and smoking hot. Most anything else is from the photos around the house and my own imagination." He let the grin smolder. "Haven't seen towels or socks strewn around, so I'm guessing you're a decently tidy person. Same."

"Oh." Finally the beer bottle got shoved aside and Galen showed a little genuine interest in the conversation, enough for a shrug. "Yeah, I guess. Mom always made sure we understood Molly was there to pick up the slack, not pick up after us." A soft snort escaped. "Knowing Molly, she'd take a broom to us even after all these years. I don't know what we'd have done, or do, without her."

Ellis nodded as he prepped two plates for the microwave. "My nanny was fucking Mary Poppins the few days each week she came in. No shit. And Mom and Dad are both slightly compulsive about order. I had plenty of role models." No great personality clash there, then. "You do any sports, or is that lacrosse stick over your bed just a weird choice for self-defense?"

"Smartass." Galen huffed out half a chuckle and Ellis felt the mood lift slightly. *We've graduated from depression to resignation. I'll take it.* "I played in college. Rowed a little. There's the mini gym over in Ben's space, complete with a boxing or kickboxing bag. I'll find a tennis match now and again." At last, some variation in the voice tone that wasn't near tears. Galen glanced at the plates. "You might want to add a little salt over those. I think he purposely only puts in about three-quarters what the recipe calls for, because his blood pressure swings and Joe pretty much douses everything anyway. But yeah, the lacrosse stick is a holdover. Pickup games are hard to come by."

Ellis felt his own chest loosen. "Check—except I suck at it, so lacrosse career ended quick. Rowing and tennis, check and check. And noted." Ellis lightly salted each plate and set the first one in the microwave. "Never tried any sort of boxing or martial arts, but it sounds interesting. Swim?"

"Not competitively, but yeah. There's the lap pool off the terrace." A rueful smile curved Galen's lips and his posture straightened enough Ellis felt lighter still. "We never did get around to the complete tour. Sorry."

"Not needed. Life's been weird." On a hunch, Ellis added a dash of pepper to the second plate as well. He'd do the first plate when it came out. "Golf?"

That got a Broadway-worthy grimace. "God, no. I leave that to Ben and Joe."

Ellis let his own laughter out. "My dad will adore them. I never could stand it. Sail?"

Galen got up to stash his beer bottle in the recycling bin, then went to the fridge and poured two glasses of ice water. "Never tried it. Wanted to." His breathing seemed to have returned to almost normal instead of the slow plodding.

"We've got a twenty-two-foot weekender for the lake. You'll love it." Having watched from a frog-on-the-counter vantage, Ellis knew where the linens and silverware were and moved to grab two settings.

Galen had returned to the kitchen island with their drinks. "And I know you cycle. You mentioned bike trails. I've never done that, but I biked everywhere from elementary through high school, even after I had my license." Now the shoulders had straightened and Galen looked as if he could move without support. Some color had returned to his face. "How about TV sports?"

"Basketball, yes. Olympics, I pick and choose through both Summer and Winter. Baseball or hockey, I'll endure it." Ellis set down the tableware as the timer beeped, and switched plates. "Please don't make me watch football."

Galen laughed genuinely this time. "I was thinking lacrosse, volleyball, and soccer. Occasionally a polo match catches my interest. We've got every sports network there is, I think."

"Polo? Like, not just water polo, but *actual* polo with horses and the shit-long croquet mallets?" Ellis shook his head, smiling. "Are you sure you're not a European prince in exile?" He crossed the short distance between them and gathered Galen close. "We've still got a couple minutes before that's done. I know a perfect way to fill that time." And a perfect way to reassure Galen that nothing between them had changed and wouldn't change.

Dinner covered a few intermediates: bucket lists, ideal dinner party guests, personal heroes. Indoor games—they seemed about even in their chess proficiency, barely average. Ellis learned that Galen would kick his ass at HALO. A good-natured debate over the best ski resort in New England followed. It was fascinating to see where they meshed and where they clashed, and to discover there really wasn't much of the latter. They'd both gone to public high schools and, for the most part, had parents who wanted productive members of society rather than entitled brats.

Ellis waited until they'd cleaned up and were cuddled on the family room sofa in front of the big brick fireplace, a gas-powered glow offering soft ambiance, before he brought up another one.

"Guilty pleasure?"

Galen glanced over at him with a rather sheepish grin. "Engineering journals and the DIY channels."

What else? Ellis laughed and twined his fingers with Galen's. "Yeah, I see why the club scene bored the hell out of you."

Galen cuddled closer, resting his head on Ellis's shoulder. "What's yours?"

Ellis considered a trite answer or the truth. No contest. "Don't have one. Guilty, I mean. Why the hell should I feel guilty over loving something because other people think it's weird?" He'd been in many an argument over that one.

Galen, however, just nodded and squeezed his hand. "Good point. Not-sorry pleasure, then."

"Any and every B-movie monster flick or Western ever made. If the effects are cheesy, I'm there. Some of them are pretty awesome." Ellis snorted and rolled his eyes toward the vaulted ceiling and the game room overlook rail above them. "And *Game of Thrones*, at least until that lame ending."

"I knew I should have warned you about that. But spoilers, you know." Galen looked up at him, the soft smile catching Ellis by the heart and hormones at the same time. "Forgive me?"

The new quip died on his tongue. "Yeah. Hold that thought." He picked up Galen's phone from the coffee

table. "Find us some slow jazz. I feel like dancing with
you again."

Slim, strong arms held him close, leading this time.
Ellis felt the last of the somber mood fade away. "Now.
Of course I forgive you. I have a feeling I'll forgive you
for just about anything." So easy to fall into each other,
to stay in this moment and forget things were about
to go to hell. Ellis pressed kisses down the curve of
Galen's neck, along his jaw, across his cheeks. "You're
not a blanket-hog, are you?"

"Mm, this is nice." Galen returned the kisses,
lingering on Ellis's earlobe. His voice vibrated softly
over Ellis's skin. "Have I stolen them yet?"

"No, but you could be lulling me into a false sense
of security." Ellis pulled Galen closer. More questions
would wait a bit. They had all night.

"I'M not sure how much chaos they're going to put me
through. Shouldn't be more than a few days, though. A
week at the most." Ellis shoved the last of his clothes
into the borrowed backpack. He didn't see much point
in retrieving the toiletries he'd use tomorrow morning
anyway, since his mother would have already made
sure new ones were sitting in his ensuite bathroom at
home. There wasn't much point in taking the clothes
either; he figured he'd be back at some point in the
near future anyway. But given he'd been missing for a
year, he ought to not *look* like he was planning to rush
back just yet. So a bag of a few clothes from a week of
recovery worked. "Your Canton trip is just for a few
days, right? How busy are you likely to be?"

"Field consults tend to be pretty intensive,
since we charge by the hour and the client pays for

accommodations." Galen seemed calmer now, lounging on the loveseat by his closet, not as ready to break. Ellis supposed the slightly extra anxiety made sense; his lover had already waded through several bouts of renewed grief over his parents the last few days, and that could be messing with his emotions over Ellis leaving when they weren't quite sure of a timeline for getting back together. "I'll probably put in a couple of ten- to fifteen-hour days and collapse into bed at night. But ProCircuit hasn't been a pissy client at any time during the process, so it should go smoothly."

"At least we'll be busy at the same time." Ellis set the duffel bag on the bench at the foot of the bed. "I figure I'll be under twenty-four-hour surveillance for at least this week. By the time you get home from Canton, I should be able to breathe enough to at least email you."

Now he dropped onto the loveseat and stretched out as best he could with his head in Galen's lap. For a few moments they simply stared at each other, Galen's fingers in Ellis's hair, Ellis wanting nothing so much as to etch Galen's face into his memory for when they were apart. He reached up to brush Galen's lips with his fingers, watching them curve into a smile, meeting it with his own.

"And cue the Hallmark Channel credits. Treat McVeigh will be sobbing into his Algonquin."

Galen glanced up at Joe, lounging in the doorway between Galen's bedroom and office with a smartass grin bright on his face. "Storey needs to lay off. Treat and I already figured out we're way too different to make it work outside of a basketball court. Thought you guys were back on your Iron Man vs. Cap fixation."

"Potty break." Joe looked them over again and shook his head. "Seriously, you two ought to be on the cover of a romance novel. Ellis, how the hell did you manage to snag him in just a week? He's usually half-Hobbit, hiding away in his hole while the rest of us are out partying."

Good thing he was. I'd have never found him otherwise. And would probably still be a frog. Ellis looked up into Galen's face again and grinned. "I can't see anything I don't like about him. And I've seen *everything*."

"Oh God. TMI. Leaving now."

"Close the door." Galen's smirk lit the room. "Nice one with the movie quote."

"I have moments of brilliance." Ellis sat up and got to his feet, pulling Galen up with him. "Now let's lock the doors and do something he would definitely consider TMI."

Chapter Eleven

ON Monday, the house felt larger than ever before. Galen had been used to rattling around it with his brothers, but now, with Ellis gone for just thirty minutes, it felt cavernous. The terrarium tucked into a corner of his room left him fighting tears every time he looked at it. Maybe he should get an actual frog or something to inhabit—

The clench to his gut had him grabbing a chair for support. He moved into his office and sat down at his desk in the client area so he didn't have to look at the terrarium anymore right now. It didn't help that the only contact information he had for Ellis was a home landline that would net him only a one-in-three chance of Ellis picking up, and an equal chance of cold-calling Ellis's mother. Which he was so not ready for. He had no idea if Ellis's father had sensed the true feelings between them, so while *that* one-in-three chance wouldn't be catastrophic, he'd have to mess around with the fucking cover story again. Thank God they'd written it down in the midst of Ellis packing what little he'd acquired while he was here, but the entire charade made Galen tired even thinking about it. But they couldn't have the parents believing Galen had taken advantage of a poor drugged-up guy who'd just escaped from his kidnapper. Bad form, that.

You'll figure it out. Or he will. Come on, you knew he had to go home for a while. He said he'd be back. He said he'd move heaven and earth to get back if he had to, if for no other reason than to return your good leather backpack. Breathe.

This was ridiculous. He had to get a grip. He'd be shoving furniture around for Molly on Wednesday; she'd know in a heartbeat something was wrong, and he had absolutely no way to drop the cover story without a million and a half questions he couldn't answer, since she hadn't met "Roland" at all. Though she might, just might, believe the fairy tale. Then he had the business trip on Thursday. In fact, Galen should have already checked his flight information and arranged a car rental. And called the ProCircuit client to see what the schedule was for the four-day consult. He could manage that much while he tried to get his bearings again.

Busywork helped. He managed an hour of travel prep and straightening up his office before the reports Ellis had been sorting out and digitizing caught his eye.

Those shouldn't be out. They should go back in the file tray until I can get to them. They should….

The emotion rose up in his throat and tried to choke him again. He strode across the length of his workspace and sank down onto the stool at his drafting table, glancing out over the lawns glistening with a touch of frost before resting his face in his hands. Too quiet, too much space by himself, too little time to say goodbye. His frog prince might as well have vanished in a puff of magic smoke. The punch to his gut felt the same.

"You got his phone number, right? Email? Address?" Ben's voice from the doorway reminded Galen to draw a breath. "New Hampshire's not that far away."

Galen rubbed his hands over his face in an attempt to not look like he was brushing away tears. "I got the home landline. He wrote down my email. Wayne smashed up his cell, so he'll have to get a new one, and I wouldn't be surprised if they call in a privacy consultant or something to...." He managed enough energy to wave a hand while he tried to pull up the right word, then gave up. "Whatever the technical term is for making sure the psycho can't get near him again." Shit, he felt drained. "Press will probably drive them crazy as well. And his family's going to be all over him for a while, what with being lost for a year and then suddenly showing up again."

"Wondered about that. He wasn't here for a week. I mean, it's a big house, but it's not that big. And his name's obviously not Roland. What's with the smokescreen?" Ben's voice was closer now, and strong fingers squeezed his shoulder. "What really happened, Galen? You said before I wouldn't believe you if you told me the truth. How weird can it be? I mean, it's not like he was invisible or popped up out of nowhere."

"Oh, you'd be surprised just how weird it could be...." Galen toyed with the idea of simply letting the whole truth out. If just one other person knew....

He wasn't sure he dared.

"Hey, by the way, what happened to Gorf? Your tank's full of plants, but no frog. What, did Joe find him loose again and dump him down the garbage disposal?" This squeeze on his shoulder vibrated slightly with a shudder. "Seriously. Tell me so I can dump a gallon of bleach down it if he did. Ew."

Oh God.... The memory of what had almost happened clenched Galen's heart hard enough he flinched. "No. No, Joe didn't... you see, it... uh...."

He looked up into his brother's gaze... and the truth came tumbling out. The whole surreal story, magick spells and human-trapped-as-frog and the pond and the gazebo and sardines and falling in love. Galen didn't stop until his voice cracked and his throat was raw, wiping tears away on the sleeve of his sweatshirt. "And now you'll be calling the guys in the white coats.... I swear, Ben, it's all true. A for-real frog prince... well, as close as we get here. It all really happened."

Ben sat very still in the conversation chair beside the drafting board that he'd moved to once Galen started talking. "Okaaay." Wide blue eyes blinked, then blinked again. Galen could watch the thought process play across his brother's face, that sharp mind so used to logic and numbers and market perceptions sorting through magick spells and fairy tales. "Um... well, I guess it could explain the suit in the gazebo. And why you'd bring a frog in the house with Captain Amphibi-Phobe around."

"I know how it sounds, Ben. I get it. But it happened. And now it's all gone." Galen got up from his drafting board, steeled his spine, and walked back to shove the stack of reports into their tray. He returned to the window end of his office. "There's nothing I can do. He's got to work all this out. And I don't know if it will work out. So I'm in love, I lost, and I'm screwed."

Ben raised a brow, some of the shock gone from his voice. "You do realize you've got far more going on with Ellis than you had with those two summer-fling flakes while you were in college, right? The ones who swore they'd write or call and never did?"

"Yeah, I know. And I know I'm probably being more than a little extra. It just feels like—It happened so fast." Dammit. He realized exactly what it felt like at the same instant the *other* familiar wave of emotion stole his voice.

"Ahh. Got it. Molly mentioned you'd had a moment the day she was here." Ben pushed up from his chair as well and closed the distance between them. A warm hand settled on Galen's shoulder again. "I'll tell you a secret. I have moments like this myself when you or Joe head off on a trip. Doesn't last long, but that 'what if' really grabs hold and doesn't want to let go. Sometimes I can power-cook through it, sometimes it takes an hour on the treadmill or the weights, and sometimes I don't breathe properly again until you walk in the door. But we can't let it rule our lives."

"I know that too. By the way, I volunteered us all to shove and lift furniture for her on Wednesday. It's too much for her by herself now." Galen sighed. "But like you said, sometimes it's fucking hard to breathe through it. Especially when I don't really know what all is in between now and seeing him again."

"Don't give up. You're better than that." Ben patted his shoulder. "Look, get the Canton trip out of the way, then give it a couple of weeks if you want to allow him time with his family. But then you figure out how to call him, write him, or drive up there and scour the entire state of New Hampshire if you have to. You make sure he knows you're not going anywhere."

Because Ben made perfect sense, he tried to shake it off, but at the moment the prospect of "not going anywhere" sat in Galen's stomach like he'd swallowed that engine he'd been working on.

A CRISP tang in the air, under a fall sky so blue it nearly vibrated, teased his senses. And a warm enough spell in late October that there wasn't any snow on the ground. Ellis paused in his bike ride down Shore Drive to listen to the mournful wail of a loon out on Lake Massabesic. Nice to be able to enjoy nature again without fear of being on the lunch menu. He wondered if Galen had gotten off on his business trip—schedules had rather gone to hell while he was staying there, and the Canton trip should have started with a flight yesterday.

His family, thank God, had really only fussed over him for three days after he got home on Monday. The checkup, which showed nothing more than a deficiency in a handful of nutrients. Having to tell the cover story about six times over—including to the police, who may or may not have believed it for all the attention Ellis paid. He thought the therapist had bought it; she hadn't prescribed much more than for him to let her know if he started having nightmares or anxiety attacks, or if anything felt off.

Not only had his parents cajoled him into *not* getting a new phone immediately, they'd been so worried about Wayne finding him again that Ellis had given in to hiring a cybersecurity consultant to go through every scrap of his electronic life and lock it down tighter than Fort Knox. Phone, email, social media, contact lists, accounts on websites he hadn't touched since he was thirteen—all purged and recreated *if* necessary. That process had started Tuesday and would take the rest of this week and part of next by itself. An image purge would take longer and likely require a sizable donation to someone at Google. Ellis figured he'd have to sit through at least one lecture from Nicole Cassin, who had more brusque efficiency packed into her five-foot-nothing frame than any guy half again her size, about all the new stuff he'd have to worry about. If Wayne really wanted to find him again, he'd probably just whip up a locator spell or something else wizard-ish, but Ellis couldn't very well tell his father or the tech lady that.

He hoped Galen would understand; they'd already discussed that things would be crazy until at least next week, and Galen would still be out of town then anyway. He'd explain it all as soon as he could.

There was the expected outrage at Wayne and plots to litigate, which he'd been utterly relieved to find wouldn't happen because there just wasn't enough evidence to do so. Making sure he ate properly and slept and was warm enough or perhaps too warm.... Finally, they'd all just let him breathe.

Today, Friday, was the first day he'd had to himself. His mother had a horse show to prepare for, and his father was either holed up in his home office or catching a golf game before the country club closed the fairways for the winter.

Ellis caught himself wondering at the level of sheer boredom. *What the hell did I do with myself before?* He honestly couldn't remember anything of substance.

Probably tennis, maybe sailing? The sloop moored at
the lake's small marina wouldn't have been put into the
boathouse for winter yet, but it didn't appeal to go by
himself. The friends he'd hung out with had moved on
with their lives. Not a one of them lit the desire to call
up and connect.

Now, if Galen were here....

*Well, he's not. Not right now. And you need to do
something about that.*

But how the hell did he show up at home after
putting his parents—well, okay, *he* hadn't put them
through it himself, but still—through the panic and
upset of his disappearance for a year, then announce
two weeks from now that he was leaving again to be
with the man he loved?

The loons and the lake had no answer for him. Ellis
sighed and pushed off, heading for the end of the bike
loop and then home.

Even after stowing the bike and grabbing a drink,
he couldn't settle. He tried sitting down with a book in
the large open area around the kitchen, solid timbers and
ceiling beams framing both an old-style keeping room
and a generous family room with its vaulted ceiling and
overlook from the second story. It was a great space for
entertaining or just hanging out, but sitting in it alone
with no noise other than the hum of the refrigerator and
some faint birdsong from outside left him wanting to
pull his hair out. And it reminded him too damn much
of the family room layout at Galen's house.

That fucking business trip. If it weren't for Galen
describing fifteen-hour workdays and hotel rooms,
he'd bike down to the marina and flirt Marco into
letting him use the phone for a few minutes. But he
didn't want to interrupt what little sleep Galen was

probably getting, and five minutes of conversation in a public place wouldn't be enough for Ellis's heart. He also didn't want Galen to think he was so clingy and needy that he couldn't handle a week's separation without calling.

He dropped the book on the solid chest, serving with its twin as a coffee table and a spot to store spare pillows and blankets, and walked over to the chess table. No move to make in the perpetual game he and his father usually had going, since they'd finished the last game before he went to New York with Wayne and there just hadn't been time to sit down and start a new one. A glance out the big windows, where a veranda with more timber and stone overlooked the stables and the small riding arena to the right and woods to the left, showed his mother putting... hmm, that one must be new, he'd have to ask its name... through its paces. He didn't feel like walking down there, either.

Upstairs was no better. He'd already straightened up his bedroom before breakfast, and now spent all of six minutes listening to a Sex Pistols album before he gave up and put the LP back into its jacket and returned it to its proper place in the rack. He managed to waste ten more minutes in the little lounge they'd renovated when he got too old for a playroom, skipping through TV channels in vain. The space was pretty cool, with its retro wallpaper on two walls and solid paint on the others, all in shades of turquoise that should have soothed, but it wasn't much fun without other people to share it with.

The back stairs took him all the way down to the basement level, the sloping property allowing for a second veranda with a patio dining area and a swing. Inside boasted another lounge area with a fireplace

and a wall-mounted TV above, a small bar area and
kitchenette, and room for a pool table and dartboard.
Absolutely none of it appealed, though he did lob a
couple of darts at the board just for the hell of it.

A guest room with ensuite bath completed the
basement living area, except for his father's office. If
nothing else, maybe he could quietly thumb through a
book if his father was working on something. Just to be
around another person.

But the office was empty, ruthlessly tidy, and silent
as well. *Guess the golf game, then.* Ellis ran absent
fingers over the framed photos, the model ships and
cars, the random interesting rocks his father picked up
while traveling.

On a whim, he pulled open a lateral file drawer,
one of the oak units holding up the bookshelves lining
three walls of the cozy room. The fourth wall extended
outward diagonally, providing a desk area with leather
client chairs for meetings with retained staff or with
friends. Floor-to-ceiling windows on all three sides of
the extension looked out over the stables and the rest of
the wooded property, the lake just visible over the tops
of the trees and stretching to the hills beyond.

Holy shit, Dad.... He'd always assumed his father
kept the files as tidy as the office itself, but investment
folders were mixed in with household accounts, legal
briefs, and what looked like random news clippings and
mementos. *It's a wonder you can find anything.* Ellis
assumed the professional files were simply copies, filed
more neatly at the lawyer's and broker's offices, but
this.... No doubt the other eleven drawers in the space
were equally chaotic. He plucked a handful of folders
from the drawer and started sorting them onto a shelf
space left empty.

His brain had a task. The torrent of thoughts and the restless vibe calmed as he lost himself in work.

"I ALWAYS wondered if perhaps one day you'd become a librarian. You certainly have a knack for order."

Ellis glanced up from his filing to find his father standing in the office doorway, golf visor and gloves still in place. "Hey, Dad. Hope you didn't have a 'system' going. I think I might have killed it."

A bemused smile lit his father's face. "Well, if I did, I have no idea what the rules were for it, so you're likely doing more good than damage." He glanced at the pile nearest, brows rising as he read the scrawled label Ellis hadn't replaced yet. "Good lord. I'd forgotten all about these." He flipped open the folder, a collection of theater playbills and tickets. "These are from when I was courting your mother. I suppose I'm rather sentimental."

"I'd say you're a romantic. You wrote in the corner of each one what she was wearing that night and if you gave her flowers or a gift of some sort." Ellis had shaken his head at that. It didn't fit the image of his father he'd had over the growing-up years. "It's a cool habit, that. Does Mom know?"

"I never thought to tell her, and I don't think she's ever snooped around down here, so perhaps not." His father removed the golf gloves, thumbed through the mementos for a moment, then closed the folder and looked at Ellis with a new twinkle in his eye. "And I suspect you could tell me exactly what Galen wore to your dinner where Dena saw you, couldn't you?"

Ellis nearly dropped the folder he held. "I—
Um…." How the hell did he answer *that*?

A quick nod and that damn smile again. "I thought
I noted a spark between you. Much more than with that
Wayne person. More than anyone you've dated before,
in fact. I realize we were all in the middle of a rather
emotionally charged situation, but you seemed content
around Galen. Grounded. For the first time in your
life, if I've been paying attention properly." His father
moved to the desk chair, dropping the visor and gloves
into the inbox tray. "The files will wait for a bit. Tell me
about him."

"He…." Okay, he hadn't anticipated this
conversation quite so soon. His parents had never been
anything but supportive, whether Ellis's current dating
interest was male or female. His father had asked this
same question more than once over the years. It just
hadn't ever set rabid bats fluttering in the pit of his
stomach before. *Maybe because Dad's right and this
is… different? Because it's real?*

"It's all right, Ellis." A broad hand beckoned Ellis
toward one of the client chairs. "Just tell me what he's
like. What you see when you look at him."

His father wasn't referring only to physical
characteristics. Ellis tried to pull his thoughts together
while he moved to the conversation area. The texture of
fine leather and cool brass studs soothed his fingertips
as he settled in the chair. "Well, he…." He'd done this
before, with any number of paramours. So why now
was it so hard to put *Galen* into words?

His father had clearly picked up on his loss for
words and decided to rescue him. "There's family
money. That's obvious. No parents around? Just the
two boys?"

Ellis grabbed on to the direct question. "Three. There's three of them. Brothers. Their folks died a few years back. Car crash outside of Manhattan during the evacuation for Sandy." He tried to remember as much as he could about the brief encounters with Ben and Joe, and what Galen had told him—after all, he was supposed to have spent several days in their home. The reality had been a little more than a week, but most of that was as a frog, so... "They run a startup company together. I mean, not that *they're* just starting up, but they help other entrepreneurs get up and running. Really well, from what I saw of their client board." Okay, that didn't sound as prattle-y out of his mouth as it had inside his head. "Ben runs the financial planning, Joe the marketing, and Galen is sort of their engineer-in-residence. He does the product tinkering and the factory consults and stuff." A grin pulled up one corner of his mouth. "They need a filing system as badly as you do, though."

His father nodded, still smiling. "So industrious. Ambitious. Some degree of compassion, clearly, as they took you in." Long fingers steepled in front of his lips. "Honesty? Integrity?"

"Oh yeah." Ellis picked up the stack of mail on his father's desk, absently sorted it, and set it back in place. "They don't need to scam anybody. They're that good at what they do." His gaze shifted out the window, the solid stonework of the stable gate giving his mind something to focus on as he voiced his thoughts. "And Galen's just.... He was puttering with an engine while I was there, something a client was having trouble with, and he got lost for hours in it. It's a joy for him, you can tell. All that 'why' and 'how' and 'what's the fix'.... He glows when he's in that zone." The memory painted itself in vivid colors across his mind's eye.

"Go on."

Now that he'd started, it was a lot easier to keep going. And there'd been enough not-sex stuff that he could give a pretty decent profile of Galen without weirding his dad out. Ellis only realized he'd gotten lost in memories and gone silent when the antique clock tucked onto a shelf chimed the three-quarter hour. He looked over at his father and served up a rueful smile on half a shrug. "Sorry. Still kind of out of it."

"No, you're not." Well shit, his dad didn't have to look *that* disbelieving and downright impish over the whole thing. "I'd say you're very much *in* it."

In.... Oh. Ellis felt his face heat, but he couldn't contain the grin. "Yeah, I guess maybe I am."

There was silence for a moment; then his father let loose the most dramatic sigh Ellis had ever heard from him, twinkle still in place. "You have absolutely no interest in taking over my portfolio, do you?" His father opened the desk drawer and removed a different sort of folder, this one black leather with gold accents. Ellis could see "Irrevocable Trust: Ellis Roland Faraday III" etched on the cover. "I had originally set this up so that you would make your own decisions on what investments you wanted to pursue, but I suspect I should change that."

Well hell, since his father had been the one to bring it up…. "Honestly, Dad, yeah, please change it. I'm not interested in it. I tried to imagine my life just playing around off the returns or whatever they're called, and I couldn't do it. I want to get my hands into life, into something… tangible? Something real, I guess, or that feels real at least. I just never really had a plan for it before now." The weight of that little secret being lifted left him feeling like he could float. "I mean, I'm sure administrative assistant or personal assistant isn't what you pictured for me, but I'm pretty damn good at it."

His father's smile widened, its light taking years off that lined face. "If the current state of my office is any indication, you are indeed pretty damn good at it." He tapped the portfolio folder. "I'll have Moira adjust the legal aspects of this, then, and put the fear of God into Dan Bannockburn to find a proper replacement at the brokerage when he retires, who can be trusted to treat you honestly. Unless your Galen and his brothers invest as well."

My Galen? Ellis tried for a nonchalant shrug and failed miserably in the wake of his own grin. Why had he been so afraid of this conversation? "Don't know about that. But they'll know when there's a good investment coming along. I think I'd like that, being able to work alongside them… I mean, if they'll… have me."

A chuckle rumbled from his father's chest. "I suspect that won't be a problem. I know we're still in the process of getting you a new cellphone and a computer we're sure is free of spyware, but the landline here still works. Nicole said it's been cleared of any trace and the new number will be fully unlisted." His dad waved off Ellis's raised brow. "Yes, call it my own paranoia, but I want you safe. So why don't you call him?"

Ellis felt the tips of his ears heat. "I, uh…. We sort of figured there'd be some rigmarole about privacy and such, so the only thing we could really do was make sure he had the old landline number. I didn't get his cell, and I can't figure out what happened to the note

I wrote his email address on. And we were kind of…
well… distracted." The heat spread to the rest of his
face at the knowing little huff crossing his father's lips.
"Um, I can probably find their consultancy website,
though."

His father nodded and started to speak, no doubt
to offer to look the consultancy up on his own laptop,
but Ellis stopped him. "He's on a business trip at the
moment, Dad, neck-deep in a consult that'll take several
days at least. Long days, hotel rooms, probably eating
like crap. And he already knows I'd need some time
here. You guys haven't seen me in a year, and Mom
would never forgive me if I left for Massachusetts right
away. I mean, hell, she's already planning that shindig
with the extended clan for… weekend after next, I
think. But yeah, after Nikki figures it's safe, I'd like to
call, or even snail-mail him if I have to." He glanced
around the office, the grin turning impish. "As soon as
I get you organized."

"TOWNSEND Consulting." The hollow quality of a
speakerphone had never sounded better.

Oh thank God. Ellis nearly kissed his new phone,
then decided Ben didn't really need to hear it. He'd
been trying for a week now to catch up with Galen. The
privacy consultant had taken the first two weeks he was
home to set up new accounts and determine Ellis had
received enough lectures to be trusted with a phone and
an email address again. But when he'd tried Galen's
business number from their website, it went straight
to voicemail and a message that the box was full. The
same thing happened the next day, and the next, and
the next. The Canton trip should have finished the first

weekend after he left, if he'd remembered the calendar correctly. Maybe he'd screwed it up? But then why no voicemail?

"Hello?" Ben's voice held both exhaustion and frustration. "Goddamn phones…. Hello?"

Oh shit. "Hey, Ben, it's Ellis. I mean Rollie. I mean Roland. I mean—" Dear God, just kill him now.

"I got it, Ellis." Okay, Ben wasn't laughing *that* hard. But the laugh seemed welcome at the moment, from the lightening of his tone. "How are you doing, man? I assume you're looking for Galen. Or are you calling to ask for my blessing?"

"I—" How the hell was he supposed to answer that? And he wasn't going to have to worry about a sweater today; the blush alone would keep him warm. "Uh, yeah, if he's around. I mean if he wants. I mean—" He stopped his own prattle this time and took a breath so his mouth would stop careening off a cliff. "Sorry. I tried calling his number, but it's been going straight to voicemail and the box is full. I'm okay. Is he okay? Does…?" *Does he still want me?* That particular question he leashed. For all he knew, Ben had no idea they were far more than friends and the blessing query had been nothing more than messing with him.

"He's fine. Well, as fine as he can be at the moment. It's been a bit of a shitshow here over the past couple of weeks. Some industrial-grade crap with a client, and the network server holding both our archives and our answering service decided to have a series of strokes in the middle of it. Our IT guy has had my balls in a sling for the past two weeks because we've never upgraded the software since we started the consulting service. They had to pull the entire archive so they can comb through it for corrupted tags."

"Oh God." It sounded ominous, and Ellis didn't even know enough about software to ask for details. *Probably for the best.* Ben sounded at the end of his rope.

"Yeah. I understand about a twentieth of what he's saying. But we're upgrading the system completely once they get through their tag-hunt, as well as investing in some redundancy software and failsafes, so it shouldn't ever happen again. But in the meantime we're back to doing it all manually. So nobody gets through unless one of us physically picks up the phone. I don't know if you tried Galen's email, but it probably got eaten. We've been scrambling like hell to keep in touch with everyone."

Ellis felt his gut start to relax. *So he wasn't just avoiding me.* "Aw, man, that sucks. Hope it's all straightened out now."

"It's getting there. Joe's made them put in an error alert so that if something fries again we'll get a robot voice telling us 'something's gone horribly wrong' and then making chomping noises. But I think they should have it back up and running by the weekend." A pause, and Ellis heard the distinct sound of a door being latched and then locked before Ben picked up the handset. "Look, Ellis, I can transfer you in a minute, but level with me first. Galen told me everything that happened. Minus the gory bedroom details, of course. But come on. A frog? Seriously?"

Okay, how much did he want to freak Ben out? Ellis opted for a soft opener. "I believe you suggested naming me Gorf after Joe tried to throw me off the upper terrace." He allowed a long moment for that to sink in, because there was no fucking way he could have known it unless he *was* the frog Ben had been looking at. "And apparently you think my name sounds like a fashion designer?"

The utter silence on the other end of the line prompted a smile. He could easily picture Ben Townsend sitting at an executive desk much like his father's, trying to wrap his modern, logical brain around magick spells. "'Kay."

Ellis decided to give him another minute or two. "Yeah. Wild stuff. Wouldn't have believed it myself if it hadn't happened to me. Good thing it wasn't Joe out by the pond that night. I'd have been roadkill and missed out on meeting a really great guy." He sobered a moment. *Oh, what the hell.* There hadn't been any hostility the night he showed up for a dinner date. "He really is great, Ben. I'm not screwing with him, I swear that to you."

"That's good." Ben seemed to have recovered from the whole sorcery deal and had switched into protective mode. "So I guess the next question ought to be, what exactly are your intentions toward my kid brother?" Or not. A smartass grin traveled over the phone line in high-def. "Or are you just calling to apply for a job as our PA?"

The brat streak was clearly a dominant gene. Ellis snorted. "God knows you need one." He sighed and took a breath. "Since he already told you everything anyway...." Wow, putting words to it for someone other than Galen wasn't as easy as he'd expected. Best to just keep it simple. "I love him, Ben. Big time. Lifetime, if he feels the same."

"Oh, I'm fairly certain he feels the same." A creak as Ben probably leaned back in his chair. "Considering he's been way off his feed ever since you left. I can't blame it all on the client chaos. So why don't you get your ass back down here with a ring and make an honest man out of him?"

Something deep in Ellis's gut went *ping*. "Do you think he'd want that? So soon? I mean, it's only been a few weeks. I thought maybe I ought to at least, you know, talk to him again to see if I should maybe, you know, come back and—" Christ, his nerves had slammed into Off-A-Cliff again.

"Ellis. Breathe." Ben's grin translated loud and clear. "Look, I know him. Hell, we've all been half parent to each other for the last six years. I saw him while you were here, and I've seen him since you left. He might be stressed out over Gyro Systems and the network mess, but that's only part of it. Half his soul is missing right now. If you're ready to take that step, I can give you ninety percent certainty—make that ninety-five—you'll get a yes in response. So put him out of his misery already."

"I, um…." His heart might never slow down at this point, but the warmth spreading through his chest and gut at the thought sure felt nice.

"Do you still want me to transfer you over, or would you rather surprise him by showing up on the doorstep?" The grin over the line had turned pure wicked now. "I can make sure he'll be home if you let me know when you're arriving."

"You're evil. My folks are going to love that." The more he thought about it, the better it felt. "Do you think I should wait and surprise him?"

"Depends how—" A sharp series of knocks stopped Ben's reply. "Hang on. Joe's out today, so this has to be Galen. Let me see what's up."

Ben laid the handset down rather than putting him on hold, so Ellis could hear bits and pieces of a tense conversation out in what he assumed was the main foyer. God, even stressed out, Galen's voice sounded so good. He wished he could be there to help.

The deep slam of the front door echoed around the office space before Ben came back on the line. "Sorry. New round of shitshow. He's gone out for a run before he punches a hole through his laptop screen."

Knowing Galen was a wreck and part of it was because of him, even if he was the smallest part, made his stomach hurt.

"I was about to say, it depends on how long you need to get it all straight in your own head and heart." The chair creaked again as Ben settled into it. "But right now I think he may need another week to get through this crap." A new grin warmed his voice. "You'll want him coherent when you propose."

Okay, so the ribbing would be part of the deal. Ellis shook his head as he smiled. "I'll keep that in mind. Fair warning: you're all likely to get semi-adopted. My dad alone will have you on the golf course every chance he gets."

"I think we can live with that. Far worse things out there than family." Ben paused, and the mood softened. "Don't make him wait too much longer, though, huh, Ellis? I'm not sure how much more of this he can take."

Ellis nodded, though obviously Ben couldn't see him. "I won't. Just have to get a handful of ducks lined up." He ran down a mental list of things he'd have to do, surprised to find it really wasn't that long. "I can probably do that week you suggested."

"M'kay. Let me give you my direct number so I can make sure he's home when you land. And I won't tell Joe, either. He'll start griping about having to rent a tux two minutes after I tell him, and Galen'll find out for sure."

Ellis wrote down the number. He'd put it in his phone as soon as they hung up. "Just, um, tell Galen I called the business line and we… only talked a minute before the thing had another stroke. Or something. Just tell him I'm all right and I'm thinking of him, okay?"

"I think that'll help his mood more than anything."

Chapter Twelve

HE was running out of time.

A month. Four weeks that felt more like fourteen. A hundred and twenty miles that could have been a thousand. Frigid winds across the lake, snow flurries, and the warmth of the ever-present goal growing closer and closer with each step he took. If only he could be absolutely sure he'd reach it.

"Ellis, hurry up. You told Ben you'd be there by six. Your mother wants to hit at least five antique shops along the coast, which is the long way around, so it's a three-and-a-half-hour drive not accounting for her browsing allotment or stopping for lunch. It's after nine now. We need to go." His father's voice filtered into the study from upstairs as Ellis gazed out the big windows.

In some ways, it felt too soon. He had only been home a month. Granted, there'd been enough activity in that month for three, but it hadn't been completely nuts. He felt truly centered for the first time in his life, with a clear purpose and direction. Even if his worst nightmare came true and Galen didn't want him, he'd have a direction to go in for a career path once his heart stopped shredding. Hell, his father would hire him while he finished his degree.

It also hadn't hurt to do an internet search and find a Wiccan lady who lived in nearby Nashua, just to see if there was a way to assure the spell had been broken and wouldn't be back. She'd informed him, more than a little archly, that Wayne was most certainly not one of them and would undoubtedly pay threefold for his foray into the dark magicks. She'd performed a cleansing ritual— and taught him to periodically refresh it himself—and confirmed the absence of any lingering dark energy. She had then supplied Ellis with a protection amulet filled with crystals and herbs. Hanging from a chain tucked under his shirt, it felt warm and comforting.

A newspaper article two days later about Wayne's apartment being found scorched and smoking from what the police were calling a bizarre ritualistic explosion, with no sign of life other than a hissing, spitting cockroach trapped in a bell jar, left Ellis believing in that Threefold Return deal. But he was still wearing the amulet, just in case.

"Ellis! Your mother is about to get out of the car and go decide what other new trinket she thinks she needs to buy on the way." His father sounded desperate now. "We're only a ninety-minute direct drive from Attleboro. It's not like you'll never see the house again."

Oh, how close he'd come to just that, though. Until a pond and a phone and a man. His mind turned to the small box in his overcoat pocket, and he pulled it out. A platinum band, the single square diamond burnished-set and framed by dual polished inlays, the inside of the ring custom-etched with pond lilies and a tiny frog in the very center. No one would ever realize just how appropriate it was. Warmth and comfort again. *Rescued by the princess. There's a nice switch.* Ellis smiled to himself at the vision of the glare he'd get for calling Galen a princess. But it was true. Their very own real-life fairy tale.

"Ellis, what on earth are you— Ah." His father stood in the doorway. "Son, you've got my files so organized I expect them to jump out on their own the next time I'm looking for something. The desk planner is color-coded for the next six months, my golf scores are in the spreadsheet, and the next time Dan comes to discuss the portfolio, I'll be ready with an argument for investing in a startup consultancy." A new warmth at Ellis's shoulder. "Galen will love that ring, and your mother will love planning a wedding. I expect they'll all be up here next week for Thanksgiving if your proposal goes well. And it will. We want to get to know our new family." The most impish chuckle Ellis had ever heard from his father puffed over the back of his neck. "As the club has closed the fairways for the winter, I'll bring the lads down here for pool and darts while she's got you and Galen picking out napkins and cummerbunds."

"Gee, thanks." Ellis closed the box and returned it to his pocket, then sighed as he turned to meet his dad's gaze. "I know it's not far. I just got thinking about…."

"Nonsense." His father grinned as Ellis's brows shot up. "You're feeling guilty because you've only been home a short while. But you're not a prisoner any longer. You can call, you can visit. We can call, we can visit. Your heart's with Galen. You should be too."

Okay, yeah, there was a little guilt, but that wasn't everything. "I just wonder if I should have told him I was planning to show up with a bunch of boxes and a bicycle in tow, instead of going with this idea of Ben's to surprise him." Ellis shrugged. "Sounds like it's been a wicked crazy month down there."

"You'll have it all sorted out for them in no time." A broad hand rested on Ellis's shoulder. "Now it's time to go, or the Pods truck you scheduled tomorrow with your things will get to Galen before you do, and your mother will have an antiquing list long enough we'll have to build an addition."

"True." Ellis had to swallow back both a laugh and a tear as he embraced his father. "Thanks, Dad."

"Of course. You're my son. I'm so very glad you've found your happy ending." His father blinked. "Such a strange phrase. It should rightly be a happy *beginning*. At any rate, you've found it. Now go keep it."

Ellis smiled. "Yes, sir."

IT was getting way too cold to sit outside in the evening. Galen shivered even in his fleece jacket and flannel-lined jeans but didn't move from the Adirondack chair under a clear, star-filled sky. The book in his lap lay open but ignored. Slow piano playing from his new phone, perched on the pond wall, did little to comfort. It just added to the incremental drowning of his soul.

The Canton trip for ProCircuit had been fine, but then Gyro Systems turned into a fucking mess. One thing after another after another. Screw Murphy's Law, it had been Murphy's Seventh Ring of Hell. A two-day consult in Seattle had turned into two weeks, with another week of remote consulting from home. Arguing with Gyro's head engineer over every single detail, having to demonstrate—twice—step-by-step things they both, or at least the Gyro guy should have, learned in their second year of engineering school.

On top of that, the website had gone absolutely ballistic, so he didn't even have the option of griping to his brothers as a release; they'd been as eyeball-deep as he had, just about different things. And two other clients had run into implementation snags, so he was still running behind and because of the holidays likely wouldn't be caught up before the end of the year. He'd barely had time to eat, slept like crap, and had absolutely no time to track down a phone number for the New Hampshire Faradays.

He knew Ellis would have to get a new phone, and his dad probably insisted on going through the rigmarole of identity protection so Wayne didn't come back to haunt them. Any social media account Ellis had before the frog… ing would have been deactivated. It made perfect sense and was something he'd have done himself, but it also meant the new information wouldn't be on a directory search yet even if he paid for the full background check. Which he'd done out of desperation during the one free evening between getting home from Ohio and the new mess that had required the intensive remote consult, then found even the home landline number matching the one he'd gotten from Ellis had been disconnected.

In fact, it looked like the whole family had gone through the identity protection routine. Calling Ellis's mom out of the blue had never been an option, but he had tried Neville Faraday's number from the background check—disconnected as well. There were no other N or E Faradays on the search results. And while New Hampshire was about the same size as Massachusetts but had only a fifth of the population, there had been several other Faradays in the area around Lake Massabesic, which included the city of Manchester, and he wasn't going to cold-call someone who *might* be a third cousin or something.

He rubbed at his temples and closed the book. *God, my head aches*.

Ben and Joe had given up trying to drag him out of his funk and were getting ready to go out for the evening. He should be sleeping… or maybe banging his head against his drafting table for the sheer stupidity of having no easy way to find Ellis again without taking a drive up there and knocking on every front door around the perimeter of the lake. And his email inbox had been eerily silent since the network came back up, though Ben had told him Ellis called the number from the website and managed to talk for all of thirty seconds before the goddamned system went haywire again. But that was a week ago, and Ellis apparently hadn't attempted it since.

Galen curled tighter into the chair, tucking his hands into his armpits for warmth. *He's stuck with his family, getting back into normal or something.* Or maybe Dad Faraday wasn't as genteel as he'd come across. Maybe Ellis really would be coerced into running the family portfolio. Maybe they'd be stuck a couple hundred miles apart for good. Maybe—

"Still an awesome setup, dude. The pond's just as nice too."

Galen whirled so fast that the lounge tilted and knocked the edge of his phone, but this time a lightning catch saved it from drowning. Ellis grinned up at him from a squat. "I am not diving for that thing this time. I never did find the first one." He straightened and tucked the phone into his own pocket, the smile no less bright. "You're supposed to be a princess."

"Ellis! Oh my God...." Galen nearly broke his neck trying to get up and around the chair. "You.... You really did...."

A strong embrace caught him before he face-planted in the cold grass, long fingers twining with his and leading him back to the lit gazebo. "Well, yeah. I said I would, didn't I?" The warm folds of a fleece blanket settled over his shoulders and those arms back around his waist. "Just shit luck the universe decided to fuck with us both at the same time."

"Oh God, I know. And I haven't had time... work's been such a wreck...." Galen gave up trying to speak, hugging Ellis tight. And then a hug wasn't enough. He cupped Ellis's face in his hands and pressed a long, lingering kiss to satin lips. "Tell me you're here to stay, please. I can't take another goodbye."

Ellis nodded, a soft smile maturing his face. "If you still need an admin."

"What? Oh." Galen drew back, letting his hands drop away from those warm cheeks. Ellis came back to work? A job? *But what about....* Galen opted for a little dignity, a half step back allowing him to pull the ends of the blanket around himself more tightly and try to not let on about the new ache in his heart matching the one in his head. "Um… yeah… I guess the guys would go for that okay…."

Ellis stared at him. Then the smile turned mischievous. "You are just too easy to prank, you know that? I'd love to work with you, sure, but that's not the only reason I came back, you dope." A lingering kiss warmed Galen's lips, soothing away the ache. "I came back to *be* with you."

"You did? I mean… you did?" It took a moment to recover.

"If you'll have me." Another kiss. "I love you, after all."

"God, yeah. I mean, I love you too. I mean, yes, I'll have you." Galen felt his face heat as he recognized that particular double-entendre. "I mean, well, yeah, that too, but I mean—"

Ellis laughed, a deep rich tenor that spread across the lawns. He pulled Galen close, stopping Galen's disjointed chatter, lacing their fingers, drawing their clasped hands against his chest. A mobile tongue explored Galen's mouth to the point the world went a little dizzy before Ellis pulled back. He stroked Galen's cheek. "You know, Ben was right to suggest I wait until I could talk to you in person. It's so fucking adorable to watch your brain outrun your mouth. I think I'll try for another round."

"What? Ben told you—" Just when he'd thought the wrecking ball in his gut had dissolved. Too soon and too easy for it to re-solidify. *It wasn't a thirty-second conversation? What the hell did they talk about? And why….* Galen glared up toward the house and realized that four figures, not two, stood on the terrace, backlit by the lights. One of them was not a male silhouette, but he recognized the other three, so the woman was most likely…. "Wait. Your folks are here? I don't understand. What's going on?"

A quick glance back at them before Ellis smiled and lifted one shoulder in a shrug. "They wanted to drive me down. And Ben's got dinner reservations for the lot of us, Which is cool by itself and all, but I thought maybe I could give us a better reason to celebrate than just being in the same acre of space for the first time in a month." He paused, pulled in a long breath that sobered the smile, and held up a small black box.

The glare vaporized and his entire world stopped, tunneling down to that box and his lover's face. "Ellis—" His oxygen backed up again and he had to consciously let it out. "Are you…?" He couldn't say it out loud or he'd jinx it for sure.

Ellis slid the gazebo's coffee table to one side and eased Galen to the edge of the bench. "Here. Gotta give Mom a good angle for her shot if this goes well." He half knelt on the bench and opened the box, turning it and holding it up so Galen could see an etched silver band with a single diamond sparkling in the gazebo lights. "Galen Townsend, will you marry me?"

Galen stared down into pale green eyes. "Ellis…."

"I really hope that's a prelude to a yes. Mom's already got appointments set up to go shopping for china patterns and auditioning deejays." Ellis's gaze twinkled. "Don't make me break her heart along with my own. Rescue me one more time, won't you?"

The ring felt cool and smooth against his fingertip in the evening air. The small diamond had been set deep enough it wouldn't catch on anything, and the beveled cuts framed it perfectly. But it could have been a rubber O-ring and he'd have been just as breathless at the sentiment. "Yes." Together, always. "God, yes!" His heart nearly reached out all on its own to pull Ellis up from the bench, drawing him close, holding him tight, never, ever letting go again.

Whoops and applause from the back terrace reached his ears. So his brothers and Ellis's parents were apparently okay with it. Galen took the ring from the box, noting the extra etching on the inner surface. "Oh, it's perfect. And I won't have to take it off or worry about it getting torn up if I have to dig into an engine. You thought of everything." He looked up into Ellis's smile. "You always take such good care of me."

"I figure we're even now. We'll just focus on taking care of each other going forward. For a long, long time." Ellis chuckled as Joe let loose with his best wolf-whistle. "Wait'll Mom drags them in for tuxedo fittings. Which she's planning to do next week. You all are invited up for the whole of Thanksgiving weekend. And I'm sure that's just the start."

"Put this ring on me first. Then I'll think about something else." The band felt cool against Galen's right ring finger. "Oh my God, that feels perfect." He wrapped his arms around Ellis's neck and kissed warm lips again. "So do you."

"I love you, Galen Townsend." Ellis pressed a kiss to Galen's forehead. "Now, I suspect they want to celebrate with us. Let's gather up your book and your phone and head inside so you can get dolled up too. We've got a dinner date. And it's too cold out here. Winter's just around the corner, you know."

Galen would never notice. Their love could keep him warm for the rest of his life.

END

Love Romance?

**DREAMSPUN
DESIRES**

Where the men are hot,
the romance is rockin',
and there's always
a happy ever after!

Like Romance
with a Touch of Magic?

**DREAMSPUN
BEYOND**

Contemporary love stories
with a paranormal twist
to make your breath catch
and your imagination soar.

Visit
www.dreamspinnerpress.com

FOR **MORE** OF THE **BEST GAY** ROMANCE

DREAMSPINNER
PRESS
dreamspinnerpress.com